◎Harcourt

Children's Books Division

REVIEW COPY

TITLE: **Kat's Promise**

AUTHOR: **Bonnie Shimko**

PUB DATE: **August 2006**
PAGES: **288**
AGES: **12 and up**
ISBN-10: **0-15-205473-1**
ISBN-13/EAN: **978-0-15-205473-1**
US PRICE: **$17.00**
IMPRINT: **Harcourt Children's Books**

Reviewers may reprint cover illustrations to
accompany reviews with the following credit:
Courtesy Harcourt, Inc.

To receive an electronic image of the cover of this book,
contact the Harcourt Children's Book Publicity Department
at the phone or fax number below.

Please send two copies of your review to:
Harcourt Children's Book Publicity
525 B Street, Suite 1900, San Diego, CA 92101-4495
(800) 221-2477 x6851   fax (619) 699-6777

Kat's Promise

Kat's Promise

BONNIE SHIMKO

Harcourt, Inc.
Orlando   Austin   New York
San Diego   Toronto   London

Requests for permission to make copies of any part of the work
should be mailed to the following address: Permissions Department,
Harcourt, Inc., 6277 Sea Harbor Drive, Orlando, Florida 32887-6777.

www.HarcourtBooks.com

Library of Congress Cataloging-in-Publication Data
Shimko, Bonnie.
Kat's promise/Bonnie Shimko.
p.   cm.
Summary: Orphaned and sent to live with her bitter
and angry aunt, thirteen-year-old Katherine learns how
her family's past has affected her and her relatives and
makes decisions about how to move forward with her own life.
[1. Orphans—Fiction.   2. Family—Fiction.   3. Family problems—
Fiction.   4. Self-perception—Fiction.   5. Aunts—Fiction.]
I. Title.
PZ7.S5566Kat   2006
[Fic]—dc22   2005033065
ISBN-13: 978-0-15-205473-1   ISBN-10: 0-15-205473-1

Text set in Janson
Designed by Lydia D'moch

First edition
A C E G H F D B

Printed in the United States of America

For my son, Rob, with love

Acknowledgments

A special thank you to my agent, Miriam Altshuler. You know how a sunny day makes you feel like smiling? Miriam's like that.

My thanks and deep gratitude to my wonderful editors, Liz Van Doren and Kate Harrison. I can't imagine having better guidance.

Hugs to Bob, Rob, and Sarah for being my family. I love you.

And thank you to Pat Peters for seeing something worthwhile in my earliest writing that I didn't even know was there. You gave me the confidence to keep going. I'll be forever grateful.

Kat's Promise

One

BEFORE I GO to sleep at night in my aunt Paulina's house, I wish that God would strike her dead. Even though a wish is nothing more than asking the air for a favor, it's the best I can do. I can't say a genuine prayer because I'm not speaking to God. Besides, I don't think he'd be very happy if I came right out and asked him to kill somebody.

I make movies in my head of tragedies that might happen to her. Lightning hits the house while I'm at school, leaving only burned matchsticks and a body that's unrecognizable. The furnace explodes while Aunt Paulina's standing next to it, counting the stacks of hundred-dollar bills I imagine she has socked away in the big black safe she keeps next to the wood bin.

Every so often I'm the cause of her death. I sneak into her room and put rat poison in the bottle of whiskey she keeps in the nightstand by her bed. Then when she goes upstairs for a nap, I take a long stroll in the park. Oh! I am so shocked and grief-stricken when I return and find her lifeless body, and the police I have called are all flustered, trying to calm me down.

There, there, they say, patting me on the shoulder with stiff, awkward hands. *Everything will be all right.* They give each other looks of desperation because none of them knows what to do with a poor orphan girl who has just lost her only living relative. Then the one that's movie-star handsome takes me by the hand and leads me into the kitchen. He sits me down at the red and white Formica-topped table, gives me a glass of milk, and offers me some cookies—as many as I want.

I'm thrilled to be rid of her. But before long, I remember it's only a movie in my head, and the heaviness returns to my heart. Then my mind drags me back a month ago to the cemetery—the day my mother was dropped into the dungeon of the earth and my soul was so dead, I wished I could be buried along with her. It is mid-November, the week before my thirteenth birthday—one of those gray Vermont days where the wind sends dead leaves scurrying across the grass like scared brown mice and the damp cold makes its way through my too-small winter coat and into the depths of me.

The piles of freshly dug earth beside the casket are covered with artificial grass, and while the preacher says the committal prayer, I hold my breath as long as I can to see what being dead feels like. It makes my head hurt, so I stop and look over at my aunt Paulina—all done up in fur, with a look of sadness on her face that is so convincing, you would actually believe she's sorry that her little sister is dead.

After the prayer, four men who work for the funeral parlor use long gray straps to lower Mama's body into the ground. Their faces strain with the weight of the solid mahogany coffin Aunt Paulina bought to prove to everybody how generous she is—the one that cost more than the operation that would have saved my mother's life.

I glance up at the clouds that look like bundles of dirty laundry hanging low against the deep violet sky and think of the preacher's words about how Mama is in the arms of the Lord now. Then I picture my mother inside that box, dressed in the worn pink suit she kept for Sunday best, and I wonder how she'll stand to be so cold when the threatening snow covers the ground. Tears that won't come grab hold of my throat and squeeze until the pain is so fierce that I can't swallow.

I think God has a mean streak like the bullies at school who steal your lunch money. It wouldn't have cost him anything to let Mama live. It's hard not to hate somebody like that.

"Come along, Katherine dear," Aunt Paulina says, as she puts her kid-gloved hand on my shoulder. "Nettie's waiting in the car. We have a long drive ahead of us."

As we're leaving, she nods and smiles at the mourners—mostly people from our church and a few of the cafeteria ladies from my school, the ones Mama worked with until the cancer ate away so much of her that she had to take to her bed. She stops to thank our across-the-hall neighbor, Mrs. McGillveray, for taking care of me after Mama died. Then she nudges me toward the shiny black Mercedes that's waiting by the cemetery gate.

"Don't!" she says when we're out of earshot. "It's bad luck to look back at a grave. I'm sure your mother taught you that."

My mother taught me lots of things, I think while we're on our way to that car. She taught me how to knit and crochet and clean a house like a professional. How to budget money so there'll still be a little left at the end of the month. And she taught me how her father disowned her because she had disgraced the family name. Then when he and my grandmother died in a car crash, he left the house and all his money to Aunt Paulina. She taught me how Aunt Paulina was in love with my father even after he married Mama, and how she'd martyred herself as a lonely spinster because of it.

And Mama *tried* to teach me to turn the other cheek

when Aunt Paulina refused to part with a penny to pay the doctor and the hospital when Mama first discovered the lump in her breast. Maybe *she* could forgive her sister's revenge, but I'm an eye-for-an-eye kind of person and I have made a promise to myself. Someday I'm going to make her pay for what she did.

"NETTIE, WAKE UP!" Aunt Paulina says, as she opens the car door. She's talking to a pale, shopworn woman with salt-and-pepper hair. She's leaning back against the seat, and her mouth, the color of a prune plum, is wide open, making loud snoring sounds. Aunt Paulina pokes her finger into the tweed wool sleeve that's covering the woman's arm, as if she's checking the plumpness of a turkey. "I hope you didn't leave the car running the whole time."

The woman snaps to attention. "Oh my!" she says, rearranging the pitiful black felt hat with the torn veil that's made its way halfway down her forehead. "I'm sorry, Miss Hanson . . . It's just that it's so cold." Then her voice begins to fade, as if the batteries are running low. "I kept turning it off, but then I'd start freezing again. I didn't . . ."

Aunt Paulina cuts the poor soul off with a look and gestures for me to get in the backseat. "I don't have time to listen to you complain, Nettie," she says. "Just get us out of here."

I can tell by the way her head drops a notch closer to her chest and the fact that she looks as if she's about to cry that Nettie is locked into my aunt's clutches as securely as I am. I wonder what hold Aunt Paulina has on this drab sparrow of a woman who should be able to fly away but seems to be trapped beneath the cat's paw.

"Katherine, Nettie's my housekeeper," Aunt Paulina says, settling herself in the passenger seat. "She'll be taking care of your needs." That's it. She doesn't do the other half of the introduction. Mama always made sure to make both people feel important.

"Hi," I say to the back of the woman's head. And then I add, "It's nice to meet you," because I know that's the proper way.

She turns in my direction and says, "I'm glad to meet you, too."

These strangers in the front seat are in charge of me now. Sometimes life has sharp edges like broken glass, and no matter how careful you try to be, you still get sliced to the bone.

"Well, let's get going," Aunt Paulina says. "It's been a long day. I'm exhausted."

I look over at Aunt Paulina with her glamour-girl face and expensive clothes and salon hairdo and wonder how God decides who gets his blessings and who goes without. The rage I feel toward him for taking my mother and then handing me over to her murderer spreads through to the core of me, and I think how if I were in charge, I would set things straight in a flash.

As Nettie cranks the key in the ignition, I see her staring at me in the rearview mirror with the kindest, bluest eyes I've ever seen—bright, clear blue like the stained-glass windows in our church when the morning sun shines through.

"Turn left at the gate, Nettie," Aunt Paulina says, as she unscrews the top of the silver flask she has taken from her purse. Then her voice climbs an octave. "Watch out for that rock! What are you trying to do . . . ruin my tire?"

The rock is so far to the right of the driveway that the car would have to leap over the curb and onto the grass to come anywhere near it. I watch as Aunt Paulina shifts in her seat, then sniffs and fingers the tight cords in her neck.

"Sorry, Miss Hanson," Nettie says in her hangdog way. "I didn't mean to be so careless." Her words sound sincere, so it surprises me when the thought of a canary teasing a hawk floats into my mind.

Aunt Paulina tips the flask to her lips and takes a long, thirsty drink. "For pity's sake, Nettie, stop apologizing and just take us home."

Nettie sits there like a tied-up dog. Then her body stiffens, and the muscles in her jaw try to punch their way straight through her skin. If my heart weren't so heavy, I'd come to her defense. I think how Mama was always surprised when I stood up for what I knew was right, while she would go out of her way to keep things on a steady course. "You not only have your daddy's good looks, Kat; you have his backbone, too," she'd say with a look of pure pride on her face. "And it's a lucky thing, because in this world, you're going to need it."

Two

WHEN WE REACH Ellenville, huge flakes of snow start to fall—miniature paper doilies. A few bold ones come ahead of the others and make you wonder if your eyes are playing tricks on you. But then, in an instant, the air is so thick with white that Nettie has to turn on the windshield wipers so she can see where she's going.

Mama used to love the first snowfall of winter. "Kat, come quick!" she'd say. "We don't want to miss it."

We'd go outside and I'd watch her twirl like a music-box dancer with her arms in the air and her face tilted toward the sky to gather the flakes on her tongue as if they were made of spun sugar. Then I'd catch her excitement and join in. That's the way my mother was. She only had to take one baby step to be pure happy about the least little thing. And she'd invite anybody around her to go along for the ride.

The clock on the dashboard reads quarter past four, and it's already getting dark when Nettie turns onto Main Street. The snow stopped as quickly as it started, and the only proof that it had actually been anything more than a flicker of a memory is a halfhearted dampness on the ground. The streetlights are dim, like they haven't decided whether to come on or not—as if maybe it won't get any darker and they can take the night off.

Ellenville is so much bigger than where I used to live. There's a whole long street of stores instead of only one block. We've already passed two gas stations, and I can see a Sunoco sign just down the road. I wonder if there'll be a little market like Chambers' General, where Mama used to send me—and a woman like Mrs. Chambers, who'd hand me a free piece of salami to nibble on while I waited for her to slice the rest.

"Be sure to get yourself something sweet," Mama would say as I was going out the door.

When I think of the coins she always tucked into my pocket so I could buy a candy bar or maybe a bag of peanuts to eat on the way home, a pang of regret cuts into my soul. Not once did I save the treat for her—not even a little bite. A desperate emptiness overtakes me when I realize that I'll never be able to tell her I'm sorry for being so selfish.

Death leaves a haunting list etched on your heart— things you meant to say or forgot or just didn't find the time for. Maybe you left them undone on purpose. Even when you know it's coming, you don't let yourself believe it—not really—because it would hurt too much. So you convince yourself that as long as everything on the list hasn't been crossed off, it can't happen.

Nettie slows the car to a crawl, then veers far to the left of the street before pulling into the driveway of an enormous white house with a wraparound front porch— a picture-book house with huge windows and double doors with thick frosted glass. We're at the end of a dead-end street with just one neighbor next door. Mama's friend Lily Beck used to live there. But she moved to Minneapolis when her son Johnny was born and left him here with her father. "Johnny has problems," was all Mama said about him. Maybe he's a juvenile delinquent.

Mama told me about her own house more times than I wanted to hear—usually after Daddy had fixed her good. I think it was the surest way she had of crawling back into her mother's arms. And when she went on about how beautiful her bedroom was with its lavender carpet and lily of the valley wallpaper, I'd make a fake fuss and tell her how pretty that sounded. The honest-to-goodness way I feel about lavender is chintzy, chintzy, chintzy—right down there with aqua and mint green. You give me a wad of cash to decorate a room, and I will head toward rich colors like navy blue and hunter green with a touch of wine red for the accent.

"What are you waiting for?" Aunt Paulina says to Nettie after she's stopped the car in front of a ramshackle garage in back of the house. The headlights are making huge yellow cat's eyes on the chipped paint. "Get out and open the doors . . . What's the matter with you? You're just sitting there."

Nettie opens the car door a crack, says nothing, and doesn't move. She looks at Aunt Paulina. The overhead light lets me see her face perfectly—a storm is brewing behind those eyes. "It's dark," she says. "I'm not getting out. You promised I'd never have to drive at night. There might be animals in there . . . snakes, even."

Pins and needles race under my skin as I wait for the blade of the guillotine to drop. But at the same time, Fourth of July sparklers light up my black mood. Maybe Nettie has a backbone after all.

Aunt Paulina grumbles something under her breath, opens her door, and walks toward the garage. When she's directly in front of the car, Nettie sits up straight and wraps her fingers around the gearshift.

A voice in my head screams, *Do it!*

The headlights make Aunt Paulina's black hair shine like satin as she throws back the doors, then twirls around; the hem of her mink coat floats through the air as if it's flying. For just a second, she looks straight at Nettie's face. But then she lowers her shoulders and runs her hands over the sparkly fur of her coat. As she's making her way back to the car, Nettie's body deflates. She lets out a sigh and stares at the empty garage.

Aunt Paulina opens the car door and peers over at Nettie. Her dark eyes snap like butter burning on the stove. "I told you there was nothing to be afraid of." Then, before she heads for the house, she says, "If I were you, snakes would be the least of my worries."

While Nettie pulls the car into the garage, a little dream runs through my head. It's about the way I would have explained the accident to the police—how Nettie's foot slipped off the brake and how she's overwrought with guilt and sadness because her best friend in the whole world is dead. I would be so convincing that the one in charge would slam the book shut and stamp it CASE CLOSED.

As we walk toward the house, a huge wave of loneliness washes over me, and I feel so sorry for myself that I want to yell at my mother for leaving me like this. I try to think of ways my life could be worse, but nothing comes. So I just go with it and let the gloom swallow me whole.

Three

"TAKE HER BAGS upstairs, Nettie," Aunt Paulina says as soon as we enter the fanciest living room I've ever seen—much nicer than the one Mama described.

I left my shoes by the back door like Aunt Paulina told me to, and I'm standing on dusty-green wall-to-wall carpet so thick that my feet have nearly disappeared. Twin velvet couches, the color of the rug, face each other in front of the red brick fireplace and surround a long glass coffee table that's holding a vase of fresh flowers. Rose brocade wing chairs stand at attention, guarding a shiny black grand piano. Deep green drapes frame the windows, and oil paintings in gilded frames hang from every wall.

The huge family portrait above the fireplace is the one thing I recognize from Mama's memories, and it draws me to it. My grandfather, wearing his black banker's suit, stands with one hand perched on the back of my smiling grandmother's chair. The grown-ups are fashionable and handsome, what you'd expect the parents of the big girl in the painting to look like—the girl with the long black curls and huge brown eyes—a model from a magazine handpicked to be their daughter. And then there's my mother with her straight sand-colored hair and plain face, as if she wandered into the wrong house. She looks like a stray dog that lands on a family's front stoop, and they decide to keep it because it's the decent thing to do.

"Do you want to come with me?" Nettie asks, looking over at me from the hall closet, where she's hanging up our coats. Her words pull me out of my trance, and I watch her close the door gently, as if it's fragile and she's afraid it might break. Then I see her reach for Mama's beautiful matched luggage her parents gave her when she graduated high school—the one nice thing she was allowed to take with her after she committed her unpardonable crime: getting pregnant with me before she married my father.

"Come with you?" I ask. *No, I don't want to come with you. I want to go home to my mother.*

"Upstairs—do you want to come with me? I'll show you where you're going to sleep."

"I guess so," I say. A chill runs down my spine that surprises me, because this room is much warmer than I'm used to. I think what a luxury it is to leave the heat on when you're gone to a funeral and there's nobody home to enjoy it. Feeding angel food cake to the devil is what Mama would call such an extravagance.

I look over at Aunt Paulina. She's busy peeling the black leather gloves off her hands. The nail polish on her long, pointed fingernails reminds me of blood, and I half expect it to rub off when she runs the back of her hand along her cheek.

If I didn't feel as if I'd been hollowed out like an old dead tree, I would take the suitcases from Nettie. Instead, I follow her up the stairs. As I watch the thick brown stockings that have fallen asleep around her ankles, Mama comes into my head. The Mama that had been so devoured by disease that her skin had gotten too big for her body—as though her bones had come unhitched and were rattling around like stones in a sack. The words she said to me just before she died echo in my memory. "I called your aunt Paulina, Kat. She came to see me and she promised to take you in. She won't let you go to an orphanage like your father had to. She'd never let that happen. You have his blood flowing through your veins. That's your ticket in. Be a good girl and do what she says."

"But I *can't* go there!" I said. My insides felt as if somebody had reached in and was squeezing tight. Then a river flowed down my face. "Please don't make me go there."

She gazed into my eyes as if she could see clear through to my soul. Tears flooded *her* eyes, and a look spread across her face like she was about to throw me to a hungry lion. She took hold of my hands, and the words fell out of her mouth—heavy as boulders. "She's all we have. Just don't cross her. When she gets into one of her moods, tell her how pretty she is. She likes that." A tiny smile now. "Everything will be okay. You'll see."

Mama stared at her hand for a long minute, then slipped off her thin gold wedding ring and folded my fingers around it. "I want you to have this," she said. "It's the only piece of jewelry I own that's worth anything."

I force my thoughts back to the staircase before Mama's dead face has a chance to sneak into my head again and remind me that people don't die with their eyes closed, looking at peace. They die in sweat-soaked beds, staring at the ceiling with frantic, hollow eyes, and their mouths frozen open like they're still gasping for their last breath. They die clutching their daughter's hand so tightly that hours later when the neighbor lady comes in, she has to peel the icy fingers away from the daughter's clenched fist.

When we get to the top of the stairs, Nettie puts the suitcases down but doesn't let go of them. Small wheezing noises escape her mouth, sounding like a cupboard door opening and closing on rusted hinges.

"Here...let me take them now," I say, slipping my hands over hers. Sandpaper flesh rubs against my fingers, and she gives me a nervous smile. I smell a familiar scent I can't identify, but it reminds me of Mrs. McGillveray.

"I'm okay," she replies, straightening herself, then rubbing the small of her back with both hands.

"I'll carry them," I say. I feel ashamed that I let this poor old woman struggle with my things. I hate that sometimes I'm mean on purpose. It's as if there's a dark corner in my heart that comes out of hiding if I'm not careful. I'm like my father in that respect, except he had an excuse. "Your daddy can't help it, Kat," Mama would say, after he'd slammed the door and left the room thick with his ugly words. "It's not his fault. The orphanage did that to him. It killed a piece of his soul."

Nettie's feet shuffle along the cream-colored hall carpet until we come to a closed door with a brass doorknob that looks brand-new. Instead of opening it, she reaches into her pocket and takes out a key. While she works to get it into the lock, the thought of what's happening grabs me by the arm—gets my attention fast. "Why is it locked?" I ask, putting the suitcases down and finally recognizing the ghost of Ben-Gay that's surrounding her.

She shakes her head, then rolls her eyes. "She keeps all the bedrooms that aren't being used sealed up. But now that you're here, she won't lock it."

I watch her shoulder blades do a dance under her pale blue dress as she struggles with the key. Finally, it cooperates and the lock releases the door from its grip.

"Well, this is it," she says, leading me into the room. "It's not much, but you'll be comfortable enough here. You have your own bathroom—that's one thing." The uncertain tone of her voice makes me think she's trying to convince herself to believe her own fib.

I'm surprised when I walk into the room, because a wrong thought told me I'd have my mother's lavender and lilies—maybe even all the nice things she left behind. Instead, I'm in a nun's room—dark wood floor, bed, dresser, nightstand, lamp—everything old and musty.

Nettie starts to hoist one of my suitcases onto the bed. "I'll help you put your things away," she says in a soft tone. Her face is loose now, and her eyes are sparkling again.

"No, that's okay. I'll do it," I say, hoping she'll give me some privacy. "There's not that much." I've already decided that I'm not going to unpack. That way I can pretend I'm just visiting—only staying a few days. A person can stand anything if there's an end in sight.

"Well, if you're sure," she says, putting the suitcase back on the floor. Then she fiddles with the lace on her collar, reaches over to touch my shoulder, and drops her voice a notch. "I just feel so bad about your mother, and I thought you might need a hand is all." She waits for me to say something, but when I don't, she gives up.

While she's walking toward the door, a snippet of guilt nips at my conscience and I try to make up for being so unfriendly. "Where's *your* room?" I ask. "Is it the one next to mine?"

Surprise covers her face. "*I* don't live here." She leaves out the *Thank god* part, but I know that's what she's thinking. "I have my own place. I only come days to do the housework, cook the meals, and drive her where she wants to go."

A jolt of disappointment smacks me hard when I picture myself alone with Aunt Paulina, and Nettie's trying so hard to be nice to me. My thoughts stumble over each other, and my words come out sounding as scared as I feel. "You come every day though, right?"

"Every day except Sunday." She massages her back again, then glances at her watch. "That's God's day." She looks over at the feeble lime-green nightstand and adjusts the lamp with the wobbly shade. "As soon as you're finished, come downstairs. I'll make you something to eat. You must be starving." She closes the door, but then opens it again. "Use the back stairs at the end of the hall. They'll take you right down to the kitchen."

As soon as she's gone, the room starts spinning, and the quivery feeling that's been running loose inside me grabs hold of my stomach, switches it into reverse, and tells me to get to the bathroom fast.

When I'm finished, I lie down on the mustard-colored chenille bedspread that's gone bald on top but still has its tufts on the sides. I look over at the matching curtains on the only window in the room and think how much I hate dingle balls. I'd like to yank them off one by one and flick them into the backyard—see if I can throw them as far as the boy who's gaping up at my window. It must be Lily Beck's son because I saw him come out of the house next door when Nettie and I were closing the garage doors. Now he's standing in the middle of the lawn bathed in the light from the back porch. He's not wearing a jacket. The cold must not bother him, though, because he's standing still as a stone and his arms are hanging by his sides like branches on a weeping willow tree.

The lamp on the nightstand casts an orange glow on the ceiling that draws attention to a water stain that's shaped like Italy. As I trace the heel of the boot with my eyes, I think how Mama always held my head when I got sick, helped me brush my teeth, and wiped my face with a damp cloth. Then she'd tuck me into bed and stay with me until I fell asleep. She had only a soft middle, no crust.

It surprises me and makes me feel a tiny bit disloyal when I realize that I just got through being sick without her. For the first time since Mama told me I'd have to come here, I don't feel like I'm going to die. I guess she was right about me being like my father. I just wish that thought didn't scare me so much.

WHEN I WALK into the kitchen, I'm surprised that it's as run-down as my room. I guess Aunt Paulina only spends money on the parts of the house she uses. Nettie's standing at the stove, stirring scrambled eggs in a cast-iron frying pan. She's wearing one of those aprons with a top and ruffles around the armholes and hem—homemade, you can tell, because it's not even, and the stitching is sloppy and the wrong color.

I can spot bad sewing because my mother taught me the right way. She could sew a dress so perfect that people wouldn't believe her when she said she made it. They would dig down the back of her neck, search for the label, and accuse her of cutting it out.

Upstairs my suitcases are filled with clothes she sewed for me that anybody would be proud to wear. When she found out she wouldn't need them much longer, she took apart her own things and fashioned them in a younger style to fit me.

I'm not as good as she was, but close. My mother taught me how to keep myself looking presentable on a shoestring. If you're careful where you shop, you can pick up fabric remnants for next to nothing. It's the buttons and zippers that run up your bill, so you save those when you outgrow something. Socks and underwear aren't worth the trouble. You buy those at Kmart when they go on special. It doesn't matter if they're a little on the dingy side. You wash them before you wear them anyway—that's a rule, because you never know if somebody might have tried them on. As far as coats and shoes, the Goodwill thrift store is the place to shop. Some people get tired of their stuff fast.

Nettie must have seen me looking over my shoulder, or else she can read my mind, because she says flat out, "Don't worry; she's gone to her room." And then the creases near her eyes fold into pleats, and her words come out on the tail end of a chuckle. "Jack Daniel's is singing her a lullaby." She keeps stirring the eggs but looks over at me with a hint of a smirk on her face, and I can hear a smile in her voice when she says, "I'm just kidding around; it's a private joke. You wouldn't understand."

I keep my face plain and don't let on that I understand perfectly. I know Jack Daniel's well. He was my father's best friend. He was the one Daddy blamed when he pounded my mother so black-and-blue, I had to call an ambulance to take her to the hospital. Then after he sobered up, he skulked past the nurses' station and into her room with his arms filled with flowers he'd picked from the neighbor's garden. He knelt by the side of her bed, bawled like a baby, and begged her forgiveness.

Oh, Mama, now's your chance, I thought as I stood on the other side of the bed, holding her hand, looking down at her battered face. *Let this be the end of it. You have all these people who know. He got careless; he didn't hide the proof this time.*

But, no. She closed her eyes, and I watched a tear fall onto her cheek and another one. Then she slid her hand over to the edge of the bed and laid it on his head, gentle as a feather.

"Do you want jelly on your toast?" Nettie's words wake me from my daydream, and I realize how good the food smells and that I'm actually hungry.

"Jelly's fine," I say, watching her spread butter over the toast. This is one of those awkward times when you don't know how to act. Maybe she likes to do things by herself. But I say what Mama would have said. "Is there anything I can do to help?"

She looks at me and smiles. "You can carry the tea over to the table and pour us each a cup," she says, cutting the toast the plain way and tilting her head toward a pale yellow teapot with a cracked spout. "I don't trust myself with it. My arthritis is giving me problems tonight—the weather, I think."

While I'm laying the pot on the table next to a vase of faded plastic flowers, I wonder if there's any part of

Nettie that doesn't hurt. Mrs. McGillveray was like that. When I made fun of one of her complaints, Mama said, "You have to be patient with her, Kat. She only wants a little tenderness. She doesn't have anyone who loves her, so her ailments get her the attention she needs. Just treat her with kindness." Then she ran her hand down my cheek and smiled. "We're the lucky ones. We'll always have each other. Don't ever forget that."

After the memory has crawled back into its shadowy corner, I realize that I don't have anybody who loves me now, either. I glance over at Nettie and think how she was once a young girl like me. And now look at her. It makes me so scared, I can't take a full breath. "I'm not hungry anymore," I say, as I head toward the stairs. "I'm sorry you went to all this trouble, but I need to go to bed."

She doesn't say anything as I walk in her direction, but her eyes tell me she understands. She reaches out like she wants to touch me, then lowers her hand to her side and fondles the ruffle on her apron instead.

When I get to my room, I put Mama's wedding ring in the nightstand drawer. I would wear it just for spite to make Aunt Paulina squirm, but I have rawboned fingers that match the rest of me. And the thought of it hidden there gives me the feeling I have money in the bank.

Mama's flannel nightgown with the rosebuds and her baby-powder scent is warm against my shivery skin. I hide my hands in the sleeves, pull my feet up, and tuck the bottom around them tight—wrap myself in a package so nothing but my head has to touch the bed linen that doesn't feel like home.

My body wants sleep, but my mind's a stubborn, jittery thing that won't leave me alone. It flits around the ugly thoughts in my head like a moth until it settles in Mrs. McGillveray's apartment, where I cried myself dry the night Mama died.

"Poor wee lamb," Mrs. McGillveray said when she found me. She hugged me to her huge, soft front and blotted her face with a wadded-up man's handkerchief. As she led me down the hall, she tapped her pale pink gums together, keeping time to the beat of a song only she could hear.

We watched from her doorway as two men took Mama's body away on a stretcher. It surprised me to see her crying, because *I* didn't feel anything. It was as if I were at the movies and some other girl's mother had just died, and these actors were following the script, pretending to look somber. It was sad, but I didn't know the person under that sheet. As soon as the movie was over, I'd go home and tell Mama all about it while we ate the supper she made when I was gone—like every Saturday afternoon.

As the actors reached the bottom of the stairs and struggled to make their way out the door, the man in the apartment below us who owns the shoe repair stepped out of his shop and held it open for them. Then he peered up at us. His face looked as if somebody had just dropped a brick on his foot. He didn't say anything, just stood there, shaking his head. Then he slapped the skirt of his brown leather apron with both hands and stepped back into his shop. I've always liked the smell of leather and shoe polish, so it surprised me when the familiar scent made me want to gag.

"There you go, pet," Mrs. McGillveray said in her slow-moving voice that's been scratched hoarse by thousands of Lucky Strike cigarettes. "Come away in and have something to eat. A nice cup of milk and a piece of sugar bread will make you feel better. In a bit we'll have a proper supper. I've a lovely boiled dinner with a ham hock simmering on the stove. Your heart'll heal faster if your belly's full." Her Scottish brogue is thick even though she's lived here for years.

Before we went into Mrs. McGillveray's apartment, she dabbed her tea-colored eyes one more time, then shoved the hanky up her sweater sleeve and nudged me in the door. The smell of cabbage hit me in the face, and someone in my head yelled at me to go home. Mama must be worried. I'm not supposed to go off without telling her.

"Here we are, love," Mrs. McGillveray said. She closed the door and led me toward the kitchen. The apartment was dim, mostly because the shades were drawn, but also because everything in it was covered with a mountain of dust. I thought how Mama always kept everything perfect. I pulled the neck of my shirt up over my nose and breathed in the soothing scent of Ivory Snow.

"YOU'LL BE COMFIER here," Mrs. McGillveray said after I told her I'd rather sleep in my own bed. "This is the way your mother wanted it. It's not right you going back in there after all that's happened. Besides, I'd feel guilty taking that beautiful sewing machine and the other things she promised me if I didn't hold up my part of the bargain."

When she leaned over to tuck in the blankets on my side of the bed, her sour breath made me blink and turn away. She must not have noticed, because she licked her thin beige lips and went on talking. "Tomorrow I'll go over and gather up your belongings. It won't hurt you to sleep in your undies for one night. In a few days your auntie will come with her fancy car and stuck-up clothes and take you on home with her."

My look must have changed to dark when she mentioned Aunt Paulina, because she stopped tucking and patted my arm. "Oh, she's a cold one, all right, but at least you'll never want for anything. I hear she's got more money than the queen herself. And it'll be in a wink of an eye that you're grown and gone. Just grit your teeth and eat as much of her steak and caviar as you can while you're there. Close your eyes and go to sleep now. Things'll look a lot rosier when the sun comes up."

I heard her slippers paddle to the other side of the bed and then a sound of clothes being tossed around. I wanted to watch, but I squeezed my eyes tight and told my brain, *No!* Then I gave myself a little talking-to about how I would feel if somebody did that to me. But my nasty self covered its ears. I opened my eyes a crack, took a peek, and had to rein myself in so I didn't cry out from the shock of what I saw. Layers of doughy flesh overlapped one another the way melting wax flows down a candle— no bones anywhere. A musty breeze hit my face as she forced a faded blue nightgown decorated with circus bears in ballet dresses over her head, then pulled it down to cover herself. As she turned toward the bed, I closed my eyes and wished I had stayed out of her business. It is hard to forgive yourself when you knew before you did a thing that it was wrong.

I expected her to crawl into bed next to me, but instead I heard her knees creak and then her tree-bark voice came out in a loud whisper. "Sweet Jesus, I'm not going to bother you with my troubles tonight because we've got more important things to talk about, but I do thank you for the delicious supper and the fact that Mr. McCowan

down at the market forgot to add it to my tab. If that's a
sin on my part, I ask your forgiveness, but he more than
likely would have thrown the ham hock to the dogs in a
day or two anyway because it was starting to turn. Besides, he's as rich as the pope, so I'm just going to count
that as a blessing and put it in the plus column, if that's all
right with you. Now, this wee sleeping child here in my
bed is another matter entirely. She needs all the attention
you can give her. I'm not going to tell you the story because I know you're the one who wrote it. But the way I
see things, now that the mess has been made, it's your job
to help clean it up, so I'm here to ask you to do that. And
I don't mean to tell you how to run your business or anything like that either, but if what you had in mind was a
tit-for-tat kind of thing, I know what you might have
been thinking. You got rid of that no-good son-of-a-bitch
father of hers, so now you think this isn't that bad. I'm
sorry I cursed right to your face like that, but you're
wrong. She and her mother had a special thing going
on between them. I've never seen any two people who
needed each other as much as they did. I'd keep her in a
minute if I thought it was the best thing for her, but she'd
wither up and die here just like everything else does. So
now it's up to you to make things turn out right for her.
Oh, and just one more thing, Jesus. Please bless her sweet
dead mother's soul, and see if you can't find an extra nice

spot for her in heaven, maybe where the sun shines all the time. Thank you for that, Lord. Amen."

Her words yanked the blinders off my heart, and a river of tears flowed down my face and onto those dancing bears. She held me and rocked me like a baby until I was all washed out and sleep pulled me into its depths.

Four

"I'D LIKE YOU to call me Mother." Aunt Paulina is sitting on the edge of my bed, brushing the bangs away from my face and speaking in a soft voice. The whiskey is still there, but it's been scrubbed and polished, so it smells almost pleasant—like butterscotch. She's wearing a gray wool skirt and a sweater the color of the cotton candy Daddy used to buy me at the county fair. Her hair is swept up into a tight knob like a ballet dancer, and the pearls around her neck match her earrings—pierced, not clip-on. The storm has blown away from her face, and it's been washed clean, just a hint of pink on her lips and cheeks to match her outfit. Her fingernails are shiny clear now.

She reminds me of the long-stemmed roses in the flower shop window back home. I think of what Mama said when I told her I liked them best. "Remember, Kat, there's a price to pay for beauty like that—the longer the stem, the sharper the thorns." I looked at her funny, like she had no idea what she was talking about. But now I would say, *Yes, I know.*

The window shade is paper-thin, so the sun told me it was time to get up hours ago. I didn't know what to do, so I stayed in bed, thinking Nettie would come. Now I hum a tune in my head to calm the nerves in my stomach and hope if I lie here long enough and say nothing, Aunt Paulina's words will crawl into a corner somewhere and die.

"Did you hear what I said?" she asks. She takes her hand back from my hair, scoots herself toward the foot of the bed a little, and wrinkles her forehead like she's examining my face with a magnifying glass. I can tell by her look that there are a lot of things about me that she is just dying to change so I will be presentable enough to walk beside her when she goes out and about.

Then I say in my head, *Whoa! There is nothing for this woman to pick apart about how I look.* I got more than my fair share in that department. It is only the finishing touches that need attention, like maybe a store-bought hair trim and a dentist to straighten my bottom teeth. I have heard comments as far back as I can remember about long blond hair and blue eyes; and even once that I was too pretty to live, whatever that means.

Then I think I may be reading her wrong. She might not be seeing me at all. Maybe it's my father's face that's in her head.

"You're *my* daughter now," Aunt Paulina says. "So I'd like you to call me Mother." She looks at me with anticipation on her face and waits for a reaction. She must think my silence means *Oh, sure, that's fine with me,* because she gets all busy around the eyes, and her voice takes on an excited, high-pitched tone. "I'll have this room done over for you—peach with cream trim is a pretty combination. We'll go shopping for clothes and then stop at Maxine's to get you a new hairstyle. A nice, short cut would show off your eyes, and we'll have to do something about those teeth. You can put that dreadful past behind and start a new life with everything your heart desires."

When I don't say anything, she stands up and walks over to the window. "I'm sorry I was cross with you yesterday. But I was sick with grief, and then the traveling and the preparations for the funeral. Well . . . I was a little on edge is all." She licks her lips and looks at me. Now it's my turn. It must be killing her that I haven't jumped at the chance to have all the things she's tried to bribe me with.

"Can I go to the bathroom?" I ask. I want to get away from her and the fact that she's treating Mama as if she didn't count for anything.

"*May* I go to the bathroom?" She looks down at me with a fake smile. "When you ask permission, you say, 'May I?'"

I know that. I just forgot. "May I go to the bathroom?"

She tilts her head and her words come out dripping with honey. "*Mother,* may I go to the bathroom?"

I set my eyes tight and stare straight into hers. "May I *please* go to the bathroom?"

"Won't you call me Mother first?"

I look at the floor and shake my head no.

The rose wilts, and its thorns are meant to cut deep when she says, "So this is the way it's going to be. Maybe you'd rather live in a foster home with a bunch of other orphans or find your own place to stay. Is that what you want?"

The worst possible thing that could ever happen to me has already happened, so she doesn't scare me. I'm not interested in luxury. All I need is a place to lay my head when night comes and a few minutes of quiet so I can read the books I'll borrow from the library. Plus a calendar to hang on the wall so I can cross off the days until

I'm grown. I look straight at her and say, "I'd rather be thrown off a cliff, burning alive, than to call you my mama's name."

She pulls back fast, then gives me an unblinking stare and flares her nose like a bull in a ring. "Fine," she says. "You'll have a roof over your head and enough to eat. That's all. The rest is up to you. Mr. Beck next door is looking for somebody to make supper and keep an eye on his idiot grandson after school. I'll call and tell him you'll be there this afternoon."

I wonder what happened to the foster home. But maybe she's saving that for when I do something even worse. Or it might be the thought of tongues wagging around town if she doesn't at least give me a chance before she throws me out onto the street.

"Get dressed," she says, careful not to look me in the eye. "And comb the knots out of that hair."

When I start to get out of bed, she looks over at me and says, "What grade are you in?"

"Eighth," I say. She wants to be my mother but doesn't even know what grade I'm in.

"Well, hurry up. It's late. I'll have Nettie show you where the school is." The starch has gone out of her voice, and she reminds me of the songs my daddy used to sing while he played his guitar. Besides his handsome face, I think it was his singing that held Mama prisoner.

She'd sit on the edge of the couch with her eyes closed and sway in time to the music, pretending, I suppose, that she was the girl he was singing about or wishing that he'd hug *her* like he did that guitar. To me, those songs sounded lonesome, like the wail of the mourning doves outside my window.

Aunt Paulina can't possibly think she'd be doing me a favor by taking Mama's place. Let's see how *she* likes favors. I reach into the nightstand drawer, take out the ring, and hold it up. "My mother wanted you to have this," I say, with fake pleasantness in my voice. "She said you'd always wanted it. Well, here it is. It's all that's left of him."

She takes the ring from my hand, rolls it around in her fingers, and her face erupts with such rage, I half expect to see smoke rise from her head. She looks over at me like I'm the dark side of the devil, but she doesn't say anything. Instead, she opens the window and throws the ring as far into the backyard as she can. Then she leaves the room in a quiet way, doesn't slam the door. This makes a bigger impression than a loud noise. I wonder where she learned that trick.

An icy wind is blowing in, so I go over to close the window. The boy from last night is rummaging around in the leaves. Today he's dressed for the weather, and as he stands up, the sun shines just right and I can see Mama's ring in his hand. When I call out to him to put it back, he doesn't look up. He pulls his head into his jacket as if he's a turtle, trying to disappear. Then he dashes toward his side of the hedge.

The cold air surrounds me like a cape, and as I look up at the clear blue sky, it doesn't surprise me to see a lone black cloud racing toward the sun.

Five

MY TEACHER'S NAME is Velma Plain, which is completely wrong for her. She is anything but plain, and it's beyond me how a mother could look down at her brand-new baby girl's sweet little face and name her something as mean as Velma. It sounds like an aftershave lotion or some kind of salve you would rub on an itch. A horrible *last* name isn't so bad for a girl because she has a chance of getting rid of it. But when it's a first name—well, a mother should be whipped for something like that is what *I* think. It wouldn't surprise me if that's the reason Miss Plain isn't married. How many men would want a person named Velma lying in bed next to them, no matter *how* pretty she is?

The Ellenville school is different from my old one. Here you don't change classes until high school, so I'll have Miss Plain for the entire day. When I find my room, it's already near lunchtime and I can see Miss Plain standing by her desk with a book in her hand. She's wearing a navy blue skirt and a white blouse with a ruffled collar. She sees me in the hall, gives me the personal touch of coming over to where I'm waiting, and introduces herself. Then she asks me my name and where I used to go to school to make me feel at ease.

I answer her questions and leave it at that. But, oh, I would love to ask if she would like to have a girl to take home with her to keep. Then I realize how foolish that would sound. She would want a new one of her own— not somebody's half-grown leftover.

When she leads me into the room, she doesn't act like most teachers when they get another kid. She doesn't call me the new girl and sigh huge as if a pukey baby has just been dropped in her lap. She introduces me and then has all the students in the class say their names so I'm not the only one on display.

"Well, Katherine," she says, adjusting a loose gold clip in her strawberry-blond curls. "There are three empty desks. You may choose any one you please."

The closest seat is right up front between two expensive-looking girls. But they're looking me up and down as if they're checking for lice. Plus, I know what's buzzing around in their heads—how they can whittle me down to a splinter with a few sugary questions like how come *I* don't have name-brand clothes and fashionable shoes? And where does my father work?

Two ordinary girls in the middle of the room smile and all but motion for me to sit between them. The dark-haired one takes her purse off the chair so it's ready and waiting. I know that's where I belong, but then I see the disheveled-looking girl in the back of the room, staring at me with indifferent eyes—the one who's sitting at the end of a whole row of boys and looks older than everybody else. The one with the unusual name. A mystery force inside my head takes me by the hand and leads me toward the empty seat next to hers. I can tell she's the kind of girl Mama would have warned me to stay away from. But there's a danger about her that draws me straight to her.

The perfect girls look relieved that I won't be contaminating their air, and the middle-row girls gape at me with their mouths hanging open as if I've just hit them with a club. Then the one with the purse slams it back onto the chair and gives me an *Okay, you've had your chance* look, and I know I've just sealed my fate.

While Miss Plain is getting back into her book, Beamer Talson is giving me the once-over in a big way. I made it a point not to look directly at her face while I was settling into my seat, because I don't know what to expect from her. Maybe she's the kind of girl who'll want to meet me in the alley after school so she can beat the tar out of me, just because that's the kind of thing she likes to do. I look at that purse sitting on the empty chair and wish for a second it were me.

THE LUNCHROOM is half where you eat and half where you have gym, so the stink of sweat interferes with the good aroma of sloppy joes. I get treated regular by the cafeteria women, not like in my old school, where Mama's friends made me feel special. When thoughts of Mama well up in my mind, I have to stop the flow of memories. This is not the time or the place to cry.

The lunch table is arranged the same as the classroom—in nests of cliques. The boys are busy shoveling food into their mouths and shoving each other around, but both groups of girls are wearing their eyes out, watching me walk toward them. You can tell their brains are sizzling and their mouths are busy whispering behind their hands like the people in the funeral parlor at my daddy's wake. Do they think I'm too stupid to notice? Mama would tell me to never mind, they don't mean anything by it, but a parade of my father's cuss words marches through my head that would shut them up in a hot second. It seems I have them riled up good. I'm a puzzle they can't solve. That's kind of funny in a way, but it makes me shaky inside to be the center of attention. Besides, I have a feeling they're discussing more than the way I look. This town is small enough that my life story has probably already been front-page news.

Beamer Talson and a greasy-haired boy with black peach fuzz on his upper lip are at the end of the table with a big space between them and the mediocre girls. They're sitting so close to each other, you'd think they were married. I guess they don't care how dorky that looks.

I take the seat opposite Beamer and put my complete attention into opening my pigheaded milk carton. When the spout finally gives way, a stream spurts across the table, and without even looking up, I know where it landed. I freeze and wait to be clobbered to death. Instead, I hear her giggle and then she says, "Bull's-eye!"

When I look over, she's wiping her face with her sleeve. She's wearing a stretched-out turtleneck under a gray blouse with a faded denim jumper over the whole business. Her face, white as a corpse, is dusted with rust-colored freckles—as if somebody flicked a paintbrush in her direction. Her pale blue eyes are fringed with light auburn eyelashes the same color as her wild bush of corkscrew hair.

"Sorry about that," I say, surprised to see her take a

pink linen napkin out of her gigantic black lunch pail—
the kind my father used to carry his supper in when he
worked night shift at the shoe factory. She dumps a pile of
waxed-paper packages onto the table and sets the pail on
the floor. Then she spreads the napkin on her lap, bows
her head, and starts to pray—out loud!

The greasy boy looks at me over huge, thick glasses
that have slid to the tip of his nose. He rolls his eyes and
blows loud air out his mouth. "She's a Catholic," he says,
with hopelessness in his voice. "Thinks she's a nun or
something."

"Don't pay any attention to him," she says, after she's
crossed herself and unwrapped a tuna fish sandwich with
the crust removed and ruffles of curly lettuce peeking
out the edges. She jabs her elbow into the boy's ribs, then
looks over at him with a smile in her eyes. "This puny
little twerp is Isaac Harper. He's the class genius, but he
doesn't have one tiny shred of common sense. Couldn't
even tie his own shoes till the third grade." Then she
reaches over and shoves his glasses up where they belong.
"If those things are going to do you any good, you have
to look *through* them." She pulls her hand back fast. "And
for crying out loud, clean them once in a while. They're
all sticky."

It was giving me a case of nerves to watch those
glasses teeter on the end of his nose, so I'm relieved to see

them where they're supposed to be. But that feeling doesn't last long, because they slide right back down, and my belly tightens again.

"You gonna eat that sloppy joe?" he says around the mouthful of pear he's working on. He's staring at my lunch like it's a hot fudge sundae.

"For god's sake, Isaac, leave her alone," Beamer says. "She hasn't even had time to pick up her fork yet." Then she looks at me and shakes her head like a frustrated mother. "I swear he's got a tapeworm ten feet long living rent-free in his gut. He'll eat anything that's not nailed down. And just look at him—nothing but skin and bones." She pushes most of her lunch in his direction, then lowers her voice. "My father packed too much as usual. Help me eat this stuff so it doesn't go bad."

The way he dives into her food, you'd never know he'd just wolfed down a complete meal.

There's a long, awkward silence while we all eat and look everywhere but at each other. Then Isaac peers over at me and says straight-out, "I hear your mother died."

I stop breathing and Beamer gives him hell with her eyes. "What's the matter with you?" she says. "You *know* you weren't supposed to mention that."

"Sorry," he says. He gathers brownie crumbs from the table, then licks them off his fingers. "It's just that mine died, too, so I know how you feel." He wipes his hand on his shirt and takes a deep breath. "Then my old man decided having a kid around was too much trouble. So before he left town, he dropped me off at school one morning and forgot to tell me he was moving. Didn't leave a forwarding address." He stares straight at me and his voice changes. "Anyway, *you* got it good. You get to live in a fancy house with that nice Miss Hanson. She's the one who gives us foster kids the best presents at Christmastime, even sends big boxes of sugar cookies with frosting from the bakery. You're lucky you got a new mother. I'd trade places with you any day."

Beamer lets out a massive sigh, then closes her eyes as if she's trying to disappear.

What he said about Aunt Paulina makes me think he must have her mixed up with somebody else, or he's just trying to get my goat. But when I look into his eyes, I can tell he's rock serious. "Yeah," I say, as if I really mean it. "You're right."

WHEN IT'S NEARLY time for dismissal, Miss Plain reaches into the top drawer of her desk and takes out a book. Then she looks back at me. "Katherine, we always finish up the day with poetry. Do you have a favorite poet?"

I start to say no, that I don't know anything about poetry, so I don't make things even worse than they already are with the other kids in the class. But then I think what difference does it make? I'm a lost cause anyway. I recognize the book she's holding, so I say, "I do like Robert Frost, but my favorite is Edgar Lee Masters." I don't add that I've read *Spoon River Anthology* a million times.

When Mama got so sick, the fear that haunted me was that she'd simply disappear into nothingness, as if she'd never been here at all. Those poems made me feel that dead people could somehow stay partly alive—could talk to the living if you just took the time to listen carefully enough.

Mama used to tell me to put that depressing book away and read something funny for a change. But she didn't know how those poems were getting my head ready for what was coming, and how much Mabel Osborne reminded me of her. In fact, the copy I neglected to return to the library on the last day at my old school is tucked safely away in my closet right now. I'd renewed it so many times that my name filled up one whole side of the card. Besides, the only other person who'd ever borrowed it signed it out before I was even born, so it isn't exactly like it's going to be missed.

"Would you like to read 'Stopping by Woods on a Snowy Evening,' Katherine?" Miss Plain asks, holding the book out for me to come take it.

"That's all right," I say, heading toward the front of the room. "I don't need the book." While I'm reciting the poem, my eyes fall on Isaac Harper's face, and it holds me prisoner until I'm finished. I try to shake the feeling that he and I are kindred spirits, but the fact that it's true takes root in my brain, and I know there's not a thing I can do to change it.

On the way back to my seat, I think how *I* have miles to go before I sleep, too. I'd forgotten for a little while that I have to go home to Aunt Paulina. And I wonder how I'm going to babysit a boy who's a head taller than I am.

Six

"It's open," I hear a man say from an upstairs window after I've pounded on Mr. Beck's door so many times, I'm about to give up and go home. There's a square of faded yellow paper taped to the doorbell that must have one time been a note that read "Out of Order," but now it just looks like a pitiful patch that's trying to keep the bell from falling off. "Come in," he says. "I'll be down in a minute." His worn-out voice matches his house, which is even bigger than Aunt Paulina's and was once what Mama called the envy of the neighborhood.

I know a little about this house because Mama told me stories about things she and Lily Beck used to do.

About the fun they had and how Lily's father was a famous writer and that they were so rich, they had maids who wore uniforms to do everything for them, even answer the door.

As I stand here looking at the peeling paint and the torn screens on the windows, I think how if *I* lived here, I'd use the broom that's leaning against the rusted glider to sweep the leaves off the porch and then pick up the candy wrappers and soda bottles. Plus, I'd untangle the lawn mower from the weeds in the front yard and push it around back. But then Mama's voice whispers in my ear to get off my high horse, that people do the best they can, and it's not my job to criticize.

As I step into the front hall, I see a white-haired man with a cane at the top of a long staircase. He's struggling to get into one of those mechanical chairs that attaches to the railing.

While he's mumbling something to himself, I'm wondering what I'll do when he falls down the stairs and kills himself. I try to do the polite thing and not gape at him. But the foyer is bare except for an empty coatrack, and I would look mental just standing here, staring at it for very long. So I inspect the cracks in the ceiling, check out a spider's web in the corner, and then look at my feet until I hear a creaky whirring sound. When I think enough time has passed, I look up and expect to see him nearly at the bottom, but I'm mistaken. If he were a racehorse, he would be barely out of the gate, and anybody who had bet good money on him would have lost it.

As he gets closer, I know most people would be thinking how much he looks like Mark Twain and leave it at that. But that's not the way my brain works. The thought that's in the front of my mind is how I wish I had a pair of scissors so I could trim his eyebrows and mustache, and a comb to smooth out his collar-length hair.

"So you're Amy's daughter," he groans, as he climbs out of the chair, then straightens himself with the help of the cane. "I'm sorry I wasn't here to answer the door. I was reading and I must have fallen asleep. I seem to do that a lot lately."

The mention of Mama's sweet name breaks me in two, and the pain must show on my face because he puts his hand on my arm and looks at me with kind eyes. "I'm sorry about your mother," he says gently. "She was a wonderful girl. It's a shame that had to happen to her after all she'd been through." He stares off at something over my shoulder and his look turns angry. "She was still just a kid for heaven's sake." Then he brushes tears away from my cheeks that I didn't even know had fallen and cradles my chin in his hand. "It's too soon for you to be out. You should go home to your grandmother. We'll manage here until you're feeling better."

His mind must be fogging over if he thinks Aunt

Paulina is my grandmother. But his tenderhearted words draw me to him, and I wish I could hold back time so I'd never have to go home. "I'll be fine," I say, trying to make my voice sound as chipper as possible. "I feel better if I stay busy."

He gives me a slow, knowing smile and nods. "Well then, why don't I show you where the kitchen is. Johnny will be home from school soon, and he'll want something to eat." He tilts his head and narrows his eyes. "You wouldn't know how to make a grilled cheese sandwich, would you? That's his favorite. I'm a complete failure in the kitchen, and he's not allowed to use the stove. Usually, I give him peanut butter and jelly, but he's getting kind of sick of them."

I'm about to tell him that I can make just about anything because Mama made it a point to teach me how to cook. But he turns and starts walking, so I follow him with baby steps.

I wonder why Johnny can't make his own sandwich. And what Mr. Beck said about him confuses me. The school is small and I didn't see that boy all day, not even during the fire drill when all the kids were together on the front lawn. "I could have walked home with him," I say, trying to make a good impression.

He stops and turns around to look at me with surprise on his face. "Didn't Paulina tell you about him? He goes to a special school and a bus brings him home. He's mentally challenged."

Oh! That never even entered my mind. But I guess it should have. "She didn't tell me much," I say, remembering the hateful name she called him. "Just that you needed some help."

"That's an understatement," he says, then laughs through his nose. When we start walking again, he picks up the pace a little.

The dining-room table is covered with tottering piles of newspapers and books—even mail that looks as if it hasn't been opened for weeks. It amazes me to see that the sideboard has escaped the clutter. It's completely bare except for a fancy silver tea set on a tray. Brown tarnish has crept over its surface like moss on a rock, but you can imagine how beautiful it must have been before Mrs. Beck died. Cancer—the down-there woman's kind, Mama said. Only Mrs. Beck died in a hospital the way people with money do.

I'm wondering what happened to the maids and the money when we enter the kitchen and Mr. Beck says, "How are you at making coffee? I can do it, but I make a heck of a mess in the process."

Then he holds up his hand to show me. I've seen old-people hands before, but never like this. The fingers are gnarled with grape-sized knots on the knuckles, and it's frozen into a fist like he's trying to hold on to an invisible ball. "Not a pretty sight, is it?" he says, turning it palm-side up and peering at it with disgust.

While he's working the muscles in his jaw, his spotted skin stretches over hollow skeleton cheeks. Then he drops his hand to his side as if he's trying to throw it away. He must have mistaken the look on my face for fear because he says, "It's not leprosy or anything like that. It's just arthritis—the kind that leaves you good for nothing."

He walks over to the table, sits down, and slides his cane under the chair. "Just poke around and find what you need. It's nice to have somebody to talk to. The days are pretty long."

Well, this is going to be awkward. I'm terrible at small talk. I look at the clock above the stove. One of the hands is gone. "The kitchen is big" is all I can think of to say.

"This used to be the happiest room in the house," Mr. Beck says. "Your mother and Lily made a lot of chocolate chip cookies here—and a lot of disasters." Then he gets a vacant look in his eyes as though he's gone somewhere else, and his words come out with loneliness attached to them. "Cook let them do whatever they wanted. I remember the time they made me a birthday cake. They couldn't have been more than six years old—both still in pigtails. The darn thing looked like a pancake covered with the most god-awful purple frosting you've ever seen in your life. Cook warned me ahead of time so I could practice being surprised, and those two little girls stood there beaming as if they'd just constructed the Taj Mahal."

Then he shakes himself awake and taps on the table with his knuckles as if he's calling a meeting to order. He clears his throat and his voice takes on a businesslike tone. "I'm sorry everything's such a mess, but we've kind of given up on trying to stay ahead of things. It takes money to keep up a house like this and, well . . . there are just too many memories to sell it."

I'm sprinkling cleanser on a grease-crusted frying pan I found soaking in the sink when he says, "I used to write books, did Paulina tell you that?"

"My mother did," I say, wishing they had a Brillo pad to hurry things along. "She told me you wrote murder mysteries."

He nods and pulls a long, raspy breath in through his nose. "I haven't written a word in two years, not since my wife died," he says, more to the air than to me. Then there's a long space of silence before he goes on. "When your mind is filled with bitterness and grief, there's no room for anything else." He sighs, then shakes his head. "But you know that as well as I do."

His words remind me of how empty I feel. I scratch at the bottom of the pan with a fork and try to think of something to say. I probably should tell him that I'm sorry about his wife, but maybe there's a time limit on the properness of that, so I stand like a dope and keep on scratching.

When *he* speaks, I can tell by his voice that he's trying to lighten the mood. "I'm sure you've noticed that things are getting a little desperate around here," he says, stacking dirty dishes on the table. "There's a story rattling around in my head, champing at the bit to get out. But as luck would have it, now that the words are back, there's nothing I can do about it. I can't even hold a pencil, let alone use a typewriter."

Before I take time to think about it, I say, "I could write it down for you." I'm drying the pan with a dingy dish towel I found hanging on a wooden rack by the sink and I wait for him to tell me I'm crazy, that he'd need a professional secretary for something that important. But the only thing I hear is the front door slam.

"I'm home, Papa!" I hear a voice call, and then footsteps race up the stairs.

"I have to tell him where I am," Mr. Beck says.

I'm about to say that *I'll* go when he holds up his hand and makes an effort to push his chair away from the table. "He'll throw one of his fits if I'm not where I'm supposed to be." He looks over at me and sees the concern on my face. "You don't have to worry," he says, reaching for his cane. "He's fine as long as everything is in its place. Any kind of change throws him into a tizzy. I didn't realize it had gotten so late."

While he's working to get out of his seat, my chest tightens, but I don't let on I hear that boy's feet racing back and forth over my head and his voice rising to a scream. I concentrate on the butter I have melting in the pan and fiddle with one of the knobs on the stove as if that's the most important part of making a grilled cheese sandwich.

By the time Mr. Beck is on his way to the door, the footsteps and the wailing have charged down the stairs and are headed our way.

"Papa! Where were you? You weren't in your chair!" The boy barrels into the kitchen, wraps himself around his grandfather like a blanket, and starts to cry. "I thought the angels came and took you away like they did Nana." Then he sees me and freezes.

"Take off your jacket, Johnny," Mr. Beck says, fumbling with the zipper. Then he looks over at me. "This is Katherine. She lives next door and came to visit us. Wasn't that nice of her? She's making you a sandwich." As the soft words flow out of his mouth, Johnny's body relaxes a bit, but he holds on to Mr. Beck's shirtsleeve like it's something valuable he doesn't want to lose. That's when I notice his shoes are on the wrong feet.

I think how my smile must look fake, like when I'm having my picture taken and don't want to be there. "Hi, Johnny," I say, not knowing what to do next.

Back home, when I was around Percy Clark, it was easy. He would just grunt and giggle, and all you'd have to do was laugh along with him and give him a piece of candy if you had one.

But this boy is different. His body is perfect—long and wiry. He has skin the color of copper and dark, curly hair. And his face is handsome enough to be on the cover of a magazine—all except his muddy eyes. It's as if God got sidetracked when he was making him and gave him the wrong ones. I think that's why he's slow. It would take an awfully long time for anything to get past those murky eyes.

"Katherine will have your sandwich ready in a minute," Mr. Beck says. "Why don't you show her that you can make your own chocolate milk." When he lays his hand on Johnny's shoulder, I see Mama's wedding ring on a string around his neck and I wonder how I'm going to get it back. Then Mr. Beck looks my way. "This guy makes the best chocolate milk in the entire world, but he won't let anybody in on the secret ingredient. Isn't that right, Johnny?"

I watch Johnny's face redden. Then he slaps his grandfather's hand away and bolts out of the room. Mr. Beck and I stand motionless as heavy thumping feet pound up the stairs and then a door slams.

I look at Mr. Beck and shrug my shoulders. "I guess he doesn't like me."

"Don't think anything of it," he says. "It's not you. It's just that he has a hard time with strangers. He'll come around."

When Johnny's snack is ready, Mr. Beck asks me to take it to him. "It's the first room on the right," Mr. Beck calls up to me as I reach the top of the stairs. I'm carrying a tray with the sandwich and a glass of chocolate milk I made with Hershey's syrup and an eggbeater to make it frothy the way Mr. Beck said Johnny likes it.

The hall is dim, but there's a river of light streaming out from below his door. When I knock, I hear frantic movement inside and then the sound of a lock. As I bend down to put the tray on the floor, he slides a piece of paper under the door and then scurries away. It's too dark to see what it is, so I fold it and put it in my pocket, then head back downstairs to get supper started.

WHEN I GET HOME, I tuck the money Mr. Beck gave me into my suitcase and take Johnny's paper out of my pocket. My breath catches in my throat when I see myself sketched perfectly. It puzzles me at first, but then I think that maybe sometimes even God is ashamed for ruining people's lives. So he throws the wrecked person a bone to make himself feel better. I wonder if Aunt Paulina is my bone. If she is, God is even meaner than I thought he was.

Seven

"It's my birthday, Mama. I'm finally a teenager," I say
to the ceiling when I first wake up. "I miss you so much."
There is a terrible longing in me to touch her live, warm
skin, lay my head on her shoulder, and feel her kisses on
my cheek. Until now I have kept my brain overloaded
with new people and getting used to a different school so
I could lock these horrible feelings out. But today is the
first Saturday I've been in this place—the empty day that
forces you to slow down, look your real feelings in the
face, and come to grips with what you've been running
from. "Can you hear me, Mama? I love you," I say, then
wait for her to answer. "Do you think Aunt Paulina knows

it's my birthday?" I get comfortable and quiet my head so I don't miss anything she has to say.

Nothing from her. If things were the way they should be, she would have tickled me awake and sung the happy birthday song and all but burst wide open with excitement, waiting for me to open my presents. And I can almost taste the delicious supper she'd make if we were back in our apartment: chicken and dumplings with candied carrots and apple pie à la mode for dessert—everything served on the good dishes. I've never been much of a cake lover, so Mama always made star-shaped holes in the pie for the candles. Then she'd carry on something fierce about making a wish before I blew them out.

Maybe Mama can see how unhappy I am and it makes her too sad to talk. I'll try to cheer her up; pretend that everything with me is okay. "Beamer Talson invited me to go to her house today," I say a little louder, just in case. "We're in the same class at school. She's older than I am because she was held back, but she's really nice and smart, too. She knows everything there is about horses. She learned that from her father." I leave out that Beamer's father works at a racetrack and his paycheck doesn't always make it home in one piece. "Oh, and she's very religious. She goes to church all the time." I don't say which church, though. Mama was a tiny bit narrow-minded when it came to that subject. Daddy used to call her a goddamn born-again Holy Roller who wouldn't know a good time if it bit her in the ass.

I'm still walking on my father's side of the street with that one. God will have to prove that he's really up there if he wants to get me back. When you pray and pray and pray and the bad thing still happens—well, you figure maybe the whole business is just a big fat joke and you're not going to let yourself be taken in again. So when your mother dies, you don't say, *Oh, okay, I didn't get what I wanted this time, so I'll set my sights a little lower—a new hair dryer, maybe.* You just get busy and try to make things turn out right yourself.

I'm out of news, so I shut up and wait for Mama to speak. The only sound I hear is the ticking of the old windup clock on the night table. It begins to pound in my head like a bass drum, and I feel like hurling it across the room. When I can't stand it a minute longer, I get out of bed and head toward the bathroom to take a shower and shampoo my hair. I want to look my best so the Talsons won't be able to take points off for sloppy hygiene. Besides, the day is just beginning, so I'll try Mama again later.

In the smart part of my brain, I realize that she can't talk to me and she isn't asleep on a soft cloud the way I try to imagine her. But if I let my real thoughts loose, they would go straight to that dark hole in the ground.

———

WHEN I GET to the kitchen, Nettie's standing by the sink, cleaning silverware and listening to the oldies station on the radio—the same one I used to listen to with Mama. She's helping Rosemary Clooney sing "Hey There." She has a dreamy look in her eye, and she's polishing a spoon to the ambling beat of the music. I don't know why it surprises me that she's a good singer. Sometimes things just don't match up.

"There's oatmeal on the stove," she says, dropping the spoon into a basin of soapy water. "Just a sec. I'll dry my hands and get you some."

"That's okay. I can do it." I open the cupboard and take out a soup bowl. Then I remember my manners and hold the dish out in her direction. "Would *you* like some?"

She puts her wet hand over her heart and says, "Me?" as if this is the first time anyone's ever offered to do something for her.

"Yes, would you like some oatmeal?"

"Well, that's real sweet of you," she says. "But I've already had mine. You go ahead and enjoy yours."

As I'm ladling lumpy paste into the bowl and thinking that a woman her age should know that you have to stir fast when you add the oats to the boiling water, Perry Como picks up the tempo with "Papa Loves Mambo." Nettie grabs a fork and attacks it as if she's in a race to see how fast she can rub the silver clear off it.

When I sit down at the table, I notice a little fluff of white tissue paper tied up with a pink ribbon next to my place mat, and my heart does a tiny somersault. It looks a lot like a present.

Nettie has stopped polishing and she's looking over at me with expectation on her face. I don't know whether to tell her that she has silver polish smeared all down one cheek. But then I think what would be the point? It would just embarrass her and make her feel foolish, like she's a little kid with jam on her face. It's not as if she's out in public where someone important could see her. Plus, sooner or later she'll discover it for herself and think that maybe nobody noticed.

I'm not sure what to do about the gift because nobody has officially handed it to me and said, *Here, this is for you.* But there she is with anxious eyes, waiting for me to make the next move, and I'm just dying to open it.

"What's that?" I ask, pointing to the package and acting nonchalant, as if I could be talking about the napkin holder. I'm good at hiding what's in my head. Living with a daddy who hits makes you an expert at molding your face to match his mood—so he doesn't decide to turn on you.

"It's nothing much," Nettie says. "Just a little something for your birthday." Then she swishes her hands around in the soapy water and shifts from one foot to the other. "Go ahead. Open it. It'll give your cereal a chance to cool."

"How did you know it was my birthday?" I ask as I'm untying the ribbon and listening to Doris Day sing "Secret Love," Mama's favorite song.

She doesn't answer, so I look over and see that she's scrubbing again. Only this time she's ignoring the slow rhythm of the music.

"Did Aunt Paulina tell you?"

At first I think she didn't hear me, but then she says, "Oh. Well, yes. Yes, she did. Before you came."

Her answer seems a little squirmy. But I don't know her very well. Maybe this is just how she is. I unwrap the paper, and there all folded up in a little square is a crisp new five-dollar bill.

"Oh, thank you," I say. "This is so nice of you. Thanks very much." I know how hard she works for her money, and I feel a tiny bit guilty taking it. But not guilty enough to give it back. "I'll put it away for something special."

"You're very welcome," she says in a pleased voice. "And if I were you, I'd spend it on something silly. After all, it *is* your birthday." She smiles. I smile back. I hope she doesn't mention Mama and how hard it must be to have my birthday without her. I have a feeling that's what's in her head, though, because she keeps looking over at me as if she's trying to decide what to do.

As I take the first bite of my oatmeal, Aunt Paulina comes into the kitchen and says, "What were you two talking about? Is it somebody's birthday?"

I take another bite—big this time so I can't talk and pretend I have to chew, which I kind of have to do because of the chunks.

"It's Katherine's birthday," Nettie says. She's rinsing the silverware now. She turns the water on full blast and makes a big racket when she drops a handful of knives into the sink.

I glance over at Aunt Paulina. She looks as if she's calculating something in her head. Then she says, "That's right. It *would* have been November." She walks over to the stove, pours herself a cup of coffee, and looks at me. "I hope you're not expecting a celebration."

She doesn't wait for a reply. She's done with me. Now it's Nettie's turn. "I assume you have money in the bank, because if you ruin my good sterling, you'll have to replace it. You're supposed to clean it one piece at a time so it doesn't get scratched."

She's such a witch. If she doesn't like the way Nettie's doing it, she should clean her own silverware.

Nettie fishes a knife out of the water and starts polishing it again. "Sorry," she says. "I'll be more careful."

Aunt Paulina takes a sip of her coffee and pulls back because it's too hot. "When you're done, leave it on the dining-room table. I'll put it away." And then she's gone—just here long enough to rain on everybody else's mood.

This is weird. "I thought *she* told you about my birthday," I say to Nettie. "Isn't that what you said?" Her slip is showing just in the back. Old people get crooked and it throws things off.

She turns slowly in my direction. "Pardon me?"

I know she heard me, but I raise my voice a little anyway. "You said that Aunt Paulina told you about my birthday."

Her face changes to a little bit desperate. "Well . . . she did."

Something is definitely fishy. "She didn't seem to know anything about it."

She folds the dish towel she's holding and unfolds it again. Then she lets out a big breath. "Maybe the booze hasn't worn off yet or she just forgot. Now finish up there so you can get over to your friend's house. You don't want to waste this nice day."

I carry my dishes over to the sink and think about pressing harder. I know how drunks are the morning after—all the mean, disgusting stuff. But their brains are usually back in gear. I guess maybe they're not all the same.

Eight

THE SIGN IN FRONT of Beamer's house reads PORTER'S FUNERAL HOME. The Talsons live in the apartment upstairs. In exchange for rent, Beamer's parents work for Mr. Porter. When he's not at the track, Mr. Talson takes care of the handyman duties and Mrs. Talson does the hair and makeup for Mr. Porter's customers.

Beamer told me her mother graduated from cosmetology school and is a bona fide makeup artist. When she was young, she had her sights set on Hollywood. There she was at the bus depot with her suitcase packed and her ticket to California in her hand when Mr. Talson burst through the door. He begged her not to go and promised her the world and the brand-new cherry-red convertible she saw in the Chevy dealer's window. Then he got down on one knee and asked her to marry him. Beamer called it romantic, but I wonder if Mrs. Talson ever wishes she were in sunny California, running her fingers through famous hair instead of sprucing up dead people and driving a used Ford station wagon.

As I'm walking around to the back door and trying to shove the memory of Mama's funeral into a dark cupboard of my mind, I hear someone whistling "When the Saints Go Marching In," and then I notice a tall, skinny man on a ladder, cleaning out a rain gutter. He's wearing brown coveralls and a wool tweed cap with the earflaps down. His face is flooded with freckles, and frizzy hair the same color as Beamer's is bursting out from under the brim of his cap.

He stops whistling and calls down, "You must be Kat. I'm Beamer's dad. She's upstairs waiting for you."

"Thanks," I say, and start walking again.

"Don't bother knocking," he says, tossing a handful of leaves to the ground. "The TV's blasting so they'll never hear you. Just go right on in and follow your ears."

"Oh, okay." I keep going.

"I'm glad you're staying for supper," he says, removing his cap and wiping his forehead with his sleeve. "I just took a couple of my world-famous custard pies out of the oven, and I've got a pot of chili on the back burner. I hope you like it spicy, because this stuff'll take the enamel right off your teeth."

"I love chili," I say. Beamer is so lucky to have a father who cooks and knows how to make a kid feel like a real person. I didn't tell her that today is my birthday because we're just beginning, but it looks as if I'm going to have a special dinner after all.

When I reach the living room, Beamer's lying on the couch, and a girl who looks about eight years old is sprawled out on a La-Z-Boy, eating potato chips. Her hair is in rollers, and her face is made up like she's been playing movie star. Beamer talks about her all the time, but seeing her surprises me. They don't look anything alike. This girl is dark haired and dark eyed and beautiful.

When I say "Hi" to get her attention, Beamer sits up fast and looks embarrassed about being so engrossed in a kiddy show.

"Cartoons are on," the little girl says in an excited voice. "Come on in and watch 'em with us. You want some potato chips? We saved that Pepsi for you—the one on the coffee table. I'm Bernadette Marie's sister, Louisa, but you can call me Weesie; everybody does. I'm seven and three-quarters. I skipped a grade, so I'm in third already. I love your hair."

Beamer shakes her head, sighs, and rolls her eyes so big, I expect to see them pop right out of her head and skitter across the thin brown carpet.

"Thanks," I say, taking a handful of chips and hoping Beamer will want to watch the rest of the show. I haven't had potato chips or Pepsi for a long time. Most of Mama's grocery money went for real food, and the closest thing to a treat in Aunt Paulina's house is a box of stale graham crackers. I have to ask permission to take one, so it's not worth the trouble.

"I didn't think you'd be here this early, so I was just killing time," Beamer says, taking the last swig of her soda. "I don't usually watch this baby stuff."

Weesie twists her face into a knot and aims it at Beamer. "You're such a big fat liar!" Then she looks at me with a teacher expression and says, "This is one of her favorite shows. She watches it all the time. She's just trying to impress you."

I'm wondering why Beamer doesn't defend herself, when she stands up, looks at me, and says, "Come on. Let's go downtown. I have some shopping to do."

"Yeah, shopping for *boys* so they can kiss you on the lips," Weesie says.

Beamer goes over to Weesie, tickles her, and makes her squeal. "I'll kiss *you* on the lips if you don't cut it out."

Weesie makes an enormous gagging sound.

"Come with me, Kat," Beamer says. "I have to tell my mother I'm leaving, and she wants to meet you." She puts on the navy-blue pea jacket she wears to school—the one that's way too big for her. Then she takes two Hershey's bars from a dish on the TV. "We can eat these later," she says, putting them in her pocket.

I'm not sure where to look when I first see Mrs. Talson because she's stark naked. She's soaking in the bathtub, and soapy water is protecting her from the waist down, but she doesn't even try to cover her top when we walk into the bathroom. She's lying against the back of the tub, reading a movie magazine, and her teetees are on display like loaves of bread in a baker's window. It surprises me that it doesn't faze Beamer at all.

I still have a boy's chest, and Mama was modest about things like that, so even when I was washing and changing her at the end, I made sure that she was covered as much as possible. It's embarrassing being here with Beamer's mother all out in the open.

To keep my eyes out of trouble, I concentrate on her long silver earrings. I can see where Weesie got her looks. Mrs. Talson could easily pass for a movie actress.

"So you're Kat," she says, scrutinizing me like I'm an outfit she's thinking about buying. "Have you been in beauty pageants before?"

"Beauty pageants?" I ask. That's the last thing in the world I'd want to do.

"Yes, like the Little Miss Chittenden County that Weesie's in this afternoon. She's got a whole shelf of ribbons and trophies from county fairs. But now we're branching out into regional competitions. You'd be in a different age category than my baby girl, so I'd be happy to get you in the next one if you want. You'd be a shoo-in with that hair and those eyes, and there's big money when you get to the state and national level." Then she rolls up her magazine and twirls it in my direction as if she's stirring paint. "Take off your coat and turn around so I can see the whole package."

"I really don't want..."

"Turn around, just let me see what you have to offer."

"*Ma,* she doesn't want to," Beamer says with disgust in her voice. "We just came in to tell you we're going downtown."

"Of *course* she wants to. She could make a million bucks with that face. Now turn around, Kat, and hoist your skirt up to your knees so I can see your legs."

I look over at Beamer for help. She pulls in a huge mouthful of air and blows it out her nose. "You might as well do it and get it over with. Otherwise, we'll never get out of here."

While I'm turning, I catch a glimpse of myself in the mirror on the medicine cabinet, and my face is as red as the sweater I'm wearing.

"Well, you've got everything, kid." Mrs. Talson sighs. "You could use some help up top, but a pair of falsies'll take care of that. All you need is a little exposure, and the Hollywood big shots will come knocking on your door with their tongues hanging out and their checkbooks in their hands."

"I'm really not interested in beauty pageants," I say, struggling to get my coat back on as fast as I can. "I'm going to be a poet when I grow up."

Mrs. Talson looks as if I've just said I'm going to drown her. "You're going to be a *what?*"

"A poet. You know, like Elizabeth Barrett Browning."

She covers her forehead with her arm and sinks lower into the water. "You mean to tell me you're going to throw away all this God-given potential and write *poems?*" Then she looks at me with absolute seriousness on her face. "I've never seen her picture, but I bet Elizabeth Barrett Browning didn't have a choice."

"We're going now, Ma." Beamer says, shaking her head. "We'll be back in time to set the table."

"Yeah, all right. Have fun. And Kat?"

"Yes?"

"At least give it some thought, okay?"

"I will," I say, smiling at Beamer as we're walking out of the bathroom. Then I wonder if she feels uneasy about all this beauty talk.

"Thank god I was born ugly," she says, as if she knows what I'm thinking. "She'd drive me nuts with that crap."

Her words sound genuine, but there's a bite attached to them that makes me think of sour milk.

"Your little sister's really something," I say on our way downtown.

"It's not her fault she's such a pain in the neck," Beamer says in a defensive tone. "My mother's trying to live her life through Weesie, and it's turning her into a spoiled brat." She stares straight ahead and the anger in her voice rears up. "That's why we're always broke. The dresses she has to wear in those stupid contests cost so much, you'd think they were made of gold. And she has to have a new one every time."

The being broke part surprises me. "But your apartment is nice," I say. "It's furnished a lot better than the one *I* used to live in."

"That stuff isn't ours." She spits the words out as if they're making her sick. "It all belongs to the Porters. They used to live in the apartment. When they built their new house, they left us all their old stuff. Mrs. Porter even brings us care packages—mostly things for Weesie and me. Every time she comes knocking on the door with bags of goodies and boxes of old clothes, I'd like to fall through the floor and disappear." She looks over at me and taps her temple with her index finger. "You saw how crazy my mother is. She lives in a fantasy world. She thinks Weesie's actually going to be a movie star some-day. That's what all this beauty pageant junk is about."

My mind goes back to what Beamer said about her mother wanting to live her life through Weesie. I bet that's what Aunt Paulina was planning to do with me. Nice try!

Beamer picks up a stick and breaks it in two. "As soon as I'm old enough, I'm going to quit school and get married. Then I can get away from her."

I give her a *What?!* look. "Don't you have to have a boyfriend for that?"

"Yeah. So? Who says I don't?"

I shrug. "Nobody. I was just wondering." There is so much I don't know about this girl.

She throws the sticks into the street—hard. "And when I have kids, I'm going to treat them all the same."

I look over at her sad face and think that I have no idea how she feels. When you are raised by a mother like mine, you know down deep in your soul that you are worth something.

When we get downtown, the streets are crowded. "What do you have to buy?" I ask on our way into Simpson's Variety Store.

"Nothing," Beamer says. "I just want to look."

"I like to do that, too," I say, thinking how Mama and I used to play the wishing game. We'd go up and down the store aisles, picking out things we'd buy if we had the money. Hers would be fingernail polish and lipstick and a new iron. Maybe even a bowl of exotic tropical fish the pet department woman would dip from gigantic tanks with a little net. Mine would be crossword puzzle books, games like Sorry! or Monopoly, a canary in a fancy cage, and a whole pound of chocolate-dipped jelly sticks. And then imaginary turkey dinners for us both in the food section, strawberry sundaes topped with whipped cream and double maraschino cherries for dessert. A five-dollar tip for the waitress to make her smile.

"Let's do the clothes first," Beamer says.

Well, this isn't what I expected. I didn't think she cared about what she wore. "Okay. Sure. That sounds like fun." I follow her to the back of the store and start checking out the jeans.

She goes over to a rack of skirts and holds out a burgundy plaid one with sewn-down pleats. "Do you like this one?"

I put back the Levi's I'm holding and walk over to her. "I love it," I say. "It would look great on you." I'm guessing here because this is the kind of skirt private-school girls wear with blazers and white blouses with round collars. I've never seen Beamer in anything but strange loose stuff that doesn't go. "Let's find a sweater to match. Then you can try them on."

She looks at me as if I've told her she can have the store. "I can't do that. This stuff is too nice."

"Sure you can. They can't stop you from trying things on." I'm not sure about that, because I've never tried on anything in a department store. But you get brave when you are with a friend.

"I don't know . . ."

"Oh, come on," I say. "Let's go. It'll be fun."

"Well, okay. But only if you try on something, too." She's smiling and there's a little bit of excitement in her voice.

Lucky for us the dressing room is empty—just a few clothes left on a rack near the door by disappointed shoppers.

Beamer's in the stall next to mine. "Are you ready?" I ask. The jeans I tried on are way too big for me. The stiff dark fabric bends funny and cuts into the back of my knees. I didn't know that denim could hurt.

There is a stark minute of silence. Maybe she's wondering why she let me talk her into this. "I guess so," she says.

Oh, good. I go into the main part of the dressing room to check again to see if we're alone. We are. "Come on out," I say. "Let's see." I rehearse a little in my head. I tell her that maybe another style would be better, to wait just a minute. I'll go take a look.

She opens the door slowly, looking as if she's afraid the audience from Carnegie Hall might be waiting for her to perform something. "I don't know," she says. "I've never worn anything this tight before."

Well, this is one of those times when I am so shocked

that my mouth freezes up. I notice her legs first. They're beautiful. She always wears her clothes so long that all you get to see are socks and shoes.

"I knew it," she says. "I look dumb." She starts to close the door.

I shove it open again. "No! You look great. I was just taking it all in." We are still so new and cautious. If we were broken in better, I would grab her by the shoulders and yell, *My god! You've got grown-up lady boobs and a tiny waist and sexy hips. Why have you been hiding all this good stuff?* Instead, I say, "You look really nice. That deep blue is perfect for you."

"You think so?"

"I *know* so." I see a three-way mirror at the end of the room. "Let's go look at ourselves."

We stand side by side. We're the same height. It's hard not to gawk at her front, all finished and perfect. Below the lame white T-shirt I chose, I can see the outline of my undershirt. I don't have anything, not even enough for a training bra. I fold my arms across my chest and hope she doesn't notice. But I don't need to worry about that. She's staring at herself hard. She runs her hand over the sweater sleeve, then holds out the pleats of the skirt and tilts her head at the mirror. "I do like this," she says. "It's nice."

I back away and sit on a nearby stool. "Turn sideways so you can see the whole thing," I say. "The skirt falls just right." While she's busy discovering her new self, I study her face. Her features are fine. It's just that there's no color. But that's not a problem. There's a whole big Maybelline section two aisles over. When we are more secure with each other, I will throw out hints. Not today, though. This is the time to concentrate on her assets.

"I wish Randy could see me in this," she says in a tiny voice. "He'd love it."

"Who's Randy?"

"What?"

"You just said you wished Randy could see you."

Color rises to her cheeks. "Nobody. Just a boy I know."

I thought Isaac was the only boy she cared about. "Is he like a boyfriend or something?"

"Yeah, he's something."

I can tell I'm not going to get anything out of her, so I stop trying. Plus, Randy's probably one of the TV actors she's so in love with.

The dreamy look leaves Beamer's face, and she steps away from the mirror. "Okay," she says, "now it's your turn."

I stand up and recross my arms. "Nah. This stuff looks awful."

"Well, the jeans don't fit, but the shirt's cute. Do you want to look for something to go with it?"

"No, let's just go. I saw a photo booth in the front of the store. We can take our pictures."

"But I don't have any money."

"That's okay," I say, thinking of Nettie's birthday gift that's tucked in my pants pocket. "I have some."

As we're leaving the dressing room, I toss the jeans and T-shirt onto the rack by the door. But Beamer zips the skirt, then positions it perfectly on the hanger and folds the sweater into a neat square. She replaces them exactly where she got them and gives them each a pat before she turns to leave.

Neither of us says anything, but I know what Beamer just learned about herself is worth a whole lot more than if she could buy every outfit in the store.

"Okay, smile," I say as soon as I've put the money into the slot in the photo booth. Beamer and I are sitting next to each other, looking straight ahead with our hands in our laps. The flash surprises us and makes us jump.

"Quick!" Beamer says. "We have to change poses." She lays her head on my shoulder. *Pow!* The light startles us again. You'd think we would have been ready for it. It makes us laugh and breaks the ice.

I throw my arm around her shoulder, make a goofy face, and wait for the next picture to be taken.

"This is the last one. Hurry! We have to do something different," I say. She puts me in a headlock and gives me a noogie. After the flash, I holler, "Ouch! Cut that out."

"Sorry," she says in a smart-ass voice. "I didn't know you had such a tender head."

I push her arm away, grab her around the neck, and noogie her twice as hard as she did me. "*Now* who has the tender head?"

"Hey! Stop it!" she yells, laughing. "What are you trying to do, start a fire?"

"Okay, you two. Out!" There's a man standing next to the booth, looking down at us with mean eyes. "Get out of there. There's no horseplay allowed in this store."

Beamer and I look at each other wide eyed. As we stand up, the photo pops out of the slot. I grab it, then follow Beamer out of the booth.

"What was all the noise about?" the man asks.

Beamer turns to him. "We were just..."

"Never mind. I don't *care* what you were doing."

I look at his dandruffy hair, his stained teeth, and the stupid-looking sweater vest he's wearing. "We're really sorry," I say. "We were just having fun."

He doesn't say anything. All his attention is on Beamer's coat pocket. It's gaping out, showing the two Hershey's bars. He reaches in and grabs them. "You have a receipt for these?"

"They're mine," Beamer says. "I brought them from home." Her words sound desperate.

"They *are* hers," I say. "She did bring them from home. I saw her."

He puts his face close to mine and drowns me with cigarette breath. "Was I talking to you?"

"No, but..."

"If you don't stop arguing with me, I'll call your father," he says. "Is that what you want?"

Well, now that's a conversation I would love to listen in on. But I don't want to get Beamer in more trouble, so I keep my sassy mouth to myself. "No," I say.

He nods, then looks back at Beamer. "I've never seen you in this store before. But we have a strict policy about shoplifting."

"I didn't steal anything," Beamer says. "I *told* you: I got those candy bars at home."

The man looks her up and down, then shakes his head. "Kid, you can't just take things. If you promise never to come in here again, I'll put this candy right back where it belongs and you can go on your way. Otherwise, I'm going to have to contact your parents, maybe even the police."

Beamer opens her mouth to say something but closes it again.

"Well... what's it gonna be?" The man stands there, fingering the knot of his ugly gray tie. He thinks he is so important—assistant to the assistant manager, probably.

Beamer's staring at her feet. "I'll go," she says. Her voice has nearly disappeared.

"Come on, Beamer," I say. "We don't want to shop here anyway." Inside I'm thinking, *You stupid jerk. I bet if she was wearing the skirt and sweater outfit, you'd be trying to give her candy.*

Mr. Big Shot holds the door open for us and watches until we're out of sight. We walk nearly a whole block in pure silence. And I am shocked when I feel my eyes fill with tears. Then huge, loud, wet sobs come out of me.

Beamer stops and grabs my arm. "What's wrong?" she says. Her eyes are frantic. "What is it? What's the matter?"

"I don't know," I say. And I don't. It's as if all the blood got drained out of me. And then something hits me smack in the heart. "That man shouldn't have treated you like that. It's not fair."

Her body relaxes a little. "He was just a dumb creep," she says. "It's nothing to cry about." She makes a silly face. "I'm the one he thinks is a thief and I'm not crying. Come on, let's go. That's my church across the street. I want to stop in for a minute and then we can shop some more. I'm not going to let that moron spoil our day."

She starts walking. I stay glued to the sidewalk. "I would have told my mother what that man did to you." I'm crying even harder now. Finally, I choke out, "Today's my birthday and I don't know how to do this without her."

"Oh god," Beamer says, "I'm so sorry." She puts her arms around me right here in the middle of Main Street and hugs me tight while I soak her shoulder. Then she waits for me to finish. She doesn't even care that people are staring at us.

———

I'M SITTING on a pew in Saint Matthew's Church, waiting for Beamer to come out of the confessional. Tomorrow is communion, and if she doesn't tell the priest every little thing she's done wrong the whole week, she can't have any.

I glance down and see that I'm still holding the photo strip from Simpson's. I study those four little pictures and realize that they tell the whole story—how our friendship grew huge in just one day. And now that Beamer is helping me carry my grief, there is a cord binding us together. A calm relief is inside me now, so I don't have to remember to breathe anymore.

I look around and see how much fancier this church is than ours at home with the plain wooden cross and no statues anywhere. I think how Beamer's sins will all be forgiven after she says her penance. I'm stuck with mine, though, because I'd have to go directly to God, and I'm still not talking to him.

IT'S NEARLY six o'clock, and Beamer and I are setting the table. Weesie's home from the pageant and is being a real pest. "I want Kat to sit next to *me*," she says to Beamer. She drags my chair to the other side of the kitchen table and makes a screeching sound on the linoleum. "I live here, too, so she's just as much my guest as she is yours." She comes back around, picks up my plate, and puts it next to hers—close. Then she rubs her hands together as if to say, *So there!* She's wearing pajamas, a tiara, and a LITTLE MISS CHITTENDEN COUNTY banner. Her makeup is smeared, so it looks as if somebody finger-painted on her face.

Beamer's standing back from the table, juggling an armful of water glasses and watching the performance. "All you had to do was say so in the first place," she says. "I would have put her over there." She looks at me. "You don't mind, do you? She doesn't spill much. Mostly her milk."

"I do *not* spill *anything*," Weesie says. "She's just making that up." She goes over to Beamer and stares at her. "Tell her you were just making that up."

Beamer tilts her head my way and in a monotone voice says, "You were just making that up."

Inside I'm laughing, but I keep a straight face.

Weesie stamps her foot hard. "Bernadette Marie, you are just so . . ."

Mr. Talson is standing by the sink, making a salad. He stops chopping celery, comes over, grabs Weesie, and turns her upside down, then tickles her stomach. This throws her into a giggle fit. Mr. Talson tips her upright and helps her readjust her tiara. "You're absolutely right. Beamer is just so *sweet*."

Weesie tightens her lips and points her finger at him. "That is *not* what I was going to say."

"Well, this is what *I'm* going to say. Go wash your face and hands. When you get back, supper'll be ready."

"Should I wake up Mom?" Beamer asks.

"She's tired," Mr. Talson says fast. "She doesn't want to be disturbed. I'll take a tray in later."

"Everything was delicious," I say to Mr. Talson when we're finished eating. "That was the best chili I've ever had."

"Why, thanks, Kat. I love to hear compliments about my cooking." He pushes his chair back. "Weesie, you clear the table. Beamer and I need to go in the living room for a minute."

"Why do you and Beamer have to go in the living room?" Weesie asks. "Is she in trouble?"

"Yup, she's in *big* trouble," Mr. Talson says. "We'll be back after I've given her a good hard spanking."

"Yeah, *right*," Weesie says. "You've never given anybody a spanking in your whole life."

"You just clear the table, Miss Nosy Britches. We'll be right back."

"Is there something I can do?" I ask as they're leaving the room.

"Nope. Not a thing," Mr. Talson says. "Today you're the guest. Next time you'll be just one of the kids and I'll put you to work big-time."

Oh, good! There's going to be a next time.

As Beamer and her dad come back into the kitchen, they tell me to close my eyes. Then they sing "Happy Birthday."

"Okay, Kat," Mr. Talson says, "you can look." There's a custard pie in front of me ablaze with a zillion candles— left over from other birthdays, because they're all different shapes and sizes. One even has a 7 on it. "Now make a wish and put out that fire before it burns the house down."

"How come nobody told *me* it was Kat's birthday?" Weesie's next to me with her arm around my neck, sitting half on my lap. "How come *I* didn't know we were having a party?"

"Because we wanted it to be a surprise," Mr. Talson says. "Now let go of Kat so she can blow out her candles."

I look at Mr. Talson's beautiful custard pie and wish for a father just like him. "That's okay," I say. "She can help." Then Weesie and I blow out all the candles in just one breath.

Nine

BELIEVE IT OR NOT, Aunt Paulina actually has friends—
two of them—the Rathburn sisters, hand-me-downs
from my grandmother, I think. Old money, Aunt Paulina
called them. I'm not sure what that means, but their family's been around so long, they named the town after
their grandmother or great-grandmother or some woman
they're related to. They're coming today for Thanksgiving dinner, and one of them called this morning and
said she hoped I'd be here because they want to meet me.
Aunt Paulina was going to do an adults-only meal and let
me eat in the kitchen with Nettie. But now I have to be
with them and try to act civilized is the way Aunt Paulina

put it. "Just sit there and answer their questions," she said. "Don't try to impress them with idle chatter."

What idle chatter? I don't plan to say anything extra. I'd rather be shot than have to do this.

Aunt Paulina and I are in a storage room. She's searching through a closet for a dress and shoes she wore when she was my age. This is the first time since I refused to call her Mother that she's had anything to do with me. Usually, she acts as if I'm invisible. She must really want to impress these women. And I'm going along with the whole thing because it's fun to see her all rattled.

"Why, they're just like new," she says with victory in her voice. She hands me a pair of not-too-bad black flats, then shakes dust off the most putrid purple velvet dress I've ever seen. She drapes it over her arm, and before I know what's happening, she yanks my sweatshirt over my head and tells me to take off my jeans.

"Why?" I ask. I try to get my shirt back, but she tucks it under her arm and I'm not about to go after it.

"So you can try on the dress," she says like I'm an imbecile. "Nettie still has time to alter it."

I'm sure Nettie would love that. Last time I saw her, she was up to her elbows, stuffing a twenty-pound turkey.

"I have perfectly nice dresses of my own," I say.

Aunt Paulina doesn't even waste words on that one. She just tells me again to get my pants off.

"I can try it with my jeans on," I say.

"But we won't be able to see..." There's a big sigh from her. "Oh, all right. Put your arms up."

She crams the dress over my head and catches my hair in the zipper.

"Ouch!" I scream. "Wait a second!" I try to untangle myself but can't.

"For crying out loud. Why didn't you hold your hair out of the way?"

"Well, you didn't give me any warning."

"Oh, never mind. Just a minute." She goes down the hall to the bathroom, comes back with a pair of manicure scissors, and snips me free. "One of these days this mop is going to go," she says.

I hold up my hair so she can zip the dress the rest of the way. "No, it's not," I say under my breath.

"We'll see about that," she says in a humdrum tone under *her* breath. Then she pulls the skirt of the dress down, stands back, and smiles. "Well, it fits perfectly. Now try the shoes."

I take off my sneakers and slide the flats on. "They're way too big," I say. "I won't be able to walk in them."

"They'll be fine," she says. "We'll stuff the toes with tissue paper. Besides, you'll be sitting most of the time. Now go take a bath and I'll come to your room later to do something with that hair. I'm not having you look like a ragamuffin in front of my friends."

I'M SITTING on the chair near my window, and Aunt Paulina's standing behind me, French-braiding my hair. "Your mother wouldn't cut her hair, either," she says, catching a tight strand with the comb. I feel like hitting her, but I don't react because I want her to keep talking. "My mother was busy with her clubs, so I was the one who had to spend hours combing the tangles out of it." Then she speaks more to the air than to me. "Nobody ever made Amy do anything she didn't want to do."

"Why not?" I ask. I touch a spot on my head where she pulled the hair so tight, it must be bleeding. "Why didn't anybody make her do stuff she didn't want to do?" She sure did enough stuff she didn't want to do the whole time I knew her.

"Because she threw fits if she didn't get her way."

"Huh" is all I say. I can't imagine my mother ever making a fuss about anything. But inside I'm glad there was a time when Mama fought back.

"Besides, she was the chosen one in our family—the genius. She always had her nose in a book." She's yanking my head around like it's my mother's and she's trying to beat it up. "Oh, our father had big plans for her." There's spite in her voice, and I don't think she's telling me what happened anymore. She's walking down memory lane all by herself, remembering out loud. "She was going to go to Harvard, be the first doctor in the family, and discover a cure for some terrible disease." Another hard twist. "That's all he talked about, how rich and famous his precious baby daughter was going to be."

Mama read a lot, but she never said anything about wanting to be a doctor. "Huh," I say again. I think how different her life could have been if all that stuff had happened.

"She loved to rub it in my face that she got better grades than I did. She even used to wave the money she got for her A's in front of my nose."

She must be making this up. Mama never said anything about being good in school. All she ever did was tell me how smart *I* was to make *me* feel special.

Aunt Paulina tells me to hold the end of the braid, then takes it back and winds a rubber band around it. "Funny how life unfolds," she says.

"What do you mean?" I ask. "Unfolds how?"

"Oh, nothing. Just that people usually get what they deserve."

Suddenly, I'm all hot inside. I turn around and look her square in the face. "What are you talking about? You don't think my mother deserved to die, do you?"

She grabs another hunk of hair and turns me back around with it. "Of course not. That's not what I meant. Now don't move. I need to get this done, and you still have to get dressed."

I can't wait till I can get away from this house.

As soon as Aunt Paulina leaves, I put on the dress and look in the mirror. It's worse than I thought it would be. The tight top and poufy hem make me look like a gigantic eggplant. I can't even breathe in this thing. But Aunt Paulina knows what she's doing when it comes to French braids. My hair looks very nice. I just wish it didn't hurt so much.

IT'S A GOOD THING Aunt Paulina's not holding a gun when she sees me walk into the dining room. I can tell by her face that I would be flat dead. I'm wearing the church dress Mama made, and my hair is its own regular combed-out self, just a little extra springy because of the braids.

The Rathburns are already seated at the table with Aunt Paulina. They're not what I expected, just regular looking and old.

"Well, this must be Katherine," the one in the red dress says. "I'm Emma." She points to the woman across from her. "And this is my sister, Baby."

The name hits me funny, and I forget my manners just long enough for Aunt Paulina to pounce. "Katherine! Miss Rathburn is speaking to you."

"Hello," I say. "It's nice to meet you." This is the iffy part. Mama said that usually women don't shake hands, but some do, so be ready. It has to be the older person's decision to go first. Nothing. Good.

"Well, don't just stand there, Katherine," Aunt Paulina says. "Sit down and join us."

"Yes, do join us, dear," Emma says. "Maybe you'll even say grace for us."

That would be easy. Mama and I always said grace before meals. But there's no way I'm going to thank God for anything. "I'm sorry," I say, "but I don't know any blessings."

Aunt Paulina glares at me while her chest rises. Then she smiles with just her mouth. The rest of her face doesn't join in. I guess she doesn't know any blessings because she says, "Emma, why don't you do the honors?"

While their heads are bowed, I think of Nettie, eating all alone, and I wish so much that I were with her.

After she's finished kissing God's feet, Emma shakes out her napkin and places it on her lap just so. Then she tilts her head in my direction and gives me sad eyes. "Baby and I were so sorry to hear about your mother's passing."

"Yes, we were," Baby says. "Such a shame, a woman her age, even if . . ."

"Baby, will you please pass the salt?" Emma says.

"But you don't use salt. Why do you want it?"

"Just pass it, please." Emma takes the shaker and puts it by her plate.

"Well, dear," Emma says, giving my hand a little bird pat, "you'll have a wonderful life here with Paulina. And it's lovely that she's going to adopt you and raise you as her very own."

"Yes, it *is* lovely and so very generous of her," Baby adds. Now *she's* pecking at my other hand with dry skeleton fingers.

I look over at Aunt Paulina. She's chewing a mouthful of something and guiding a mound of cranberry sauce onto the back of her fork with her knife. Her eyes are down, so the satisfaction she must be feeling doesn't show.

My whole body goes cold. Can somebody do that? Adopt a person that doesn't want to be adopted?

"Just think," Emma says, "you'll have everything you've ever wanted."

Not if the person who doesn't want to be adopted runs away.

"And you'll be able to hold your head up high when you introduce her as your mother," Baby says. "Not like how it must have been before." She shakes her head and makes a clucking sound with her tongue.

"What do you mean, how it was before?" I say. "It was *perfect* before."

"Baby, stop," Emma pleads. She looks at me and lowers her voice. "You'll have to forgive my sister. She's had some small ... well ... spells, and she's not as discreet as she used to be." I can tell by Emma's phony voice that she's enjoying this.

"I haven't had any *spells*," Baby says. "I just tell the truth. And Amy Hanson had no morals whatsoever. Nice young ladies don't get pregnant *before* they're married. Shame on her!"

Shame on you for being so mean, you miserable old hag. I can't believe what's happening. It's as if Mama's being attacked by a bunch of evil-mouthed vultures.

"Anyway, dear, you're in good hands now," Emma says, like I've been yanked from the arms of the devil.

Baby starts talking to the napkin she's winding around her thumb. "And after she pulled that disgusting stunt, she turned right around and killed her parents."

I guess this woman really *is* crazy.

Aunt Paulina's pretending to concentrate on her plate, but I can still see the smirk on her face.

Emma glances at me, then at her sister. "What on earth are you talking about?"

Baby purses her lips at Emma. "You know as well as I do. The only reason they went to Florida was to get away from the scandal. And then on the way home . . . that horrible accident. She might as well have slit their throats."

I don't remember pushing my chair away from the table, but I'm standing and some of my father's favorite words spew out of my mouth. "You can all go straight to hell. You're nothing but a bunch of goddamn bitches. My mother had more goodness in her than all of you put together." I look over at Aunt Paulina. She's holding her fork in midair, staring at me like I'm a circus freak. "And there's no way I'm going to let you adopt me."

Then there it is—the flood of tears that comes after the dam breaks. I drop my napkin on the chair and run toward the stairs. I know I'll have to pay for what I just did. And when I do, it'll be with interest. When I get to my room, I'm shaking so badly, I have to lie down so I don't keel over.

Ten

"Cut her hair short, Helen," Aunt Paulina tells the beautician at Maxine's. I'm sitting in her chair, looking at myself in the mirror, and feeling sick to my stomach. This is one of those times when you can't believe how bad a mess you got yourself into.

The shop is done up for Christmas. Faded cardboard cutouts are taped here and there, and garlands of thread-bare tinsel drape the mirrors. It surprises me that Aunt Paulina comes to such a cheesy place to have her hair done. But I guess when you live in a small town, you take what you can get, even if you can afford to buy the place and burn it down.

My mother never had the money to pay a professional to fuss with her hair. She managed it herself until I was old enough to cut it and give her home permanents. And I loved it when she washed mine and brushed it so gently, it were as if she were handling air.

There's a radio in the corner and some old-time singer is crooning "I'll Be Home for Christmas." I rest my nose on my fist and pretend it's the permanent solution on the woman in the next chair that's making my eyes water. Helen can see through me, but she doesn't know it's the song that's making me cry. She leans in close and says, "Is that okay with you, honey? How long since you had it cut?" Her breath smells like coffee and something else, an onion bagel, maybe.

"Never," I say, wiping my eyes with the Kleenex she handed me. "My mother just trimmed it once in a while."

Helen digs into the neck of her uniform and rescues the runaway bra strap that's hanging out her sleeve—a thin, gray snake of a thing. Then she looks over at Aunt Paulina and holds out a clump of my hair. "Miss Hanson, are you sure about this? It'd be a crying shame to cut all this off." She pulls the strands apart, lays them across her hand, and pets them like you would a kitten. "I don't think I've ever seen such beautiful hair, so thick and healthy with the natural streaks and all. How about just an inch or two—to even it up?"

Aunt Paulina gets out of her chair, tosses the magazine she was reading back onto the table, and walks toward us, laughing in a forced way. "It's just *hair,* Helen. She can let it grow back if she doesn't like it. Besides, it was her idea." I'm staring at the rattail combs drowning in the jar of blue Barbacide on the counter when she catches my eye in the mirror and puts her hand on my shoulder, ready for action. "Isn't that right, Katherine?"

I sit here looking at the pasted-on smile she uses to confuse people—the one she can pluck from the air as easily as a magician pulls a dove out of his sleeve—and I wish she'd choke to death on the lie.

I'd like to tell Helen what this is really about—that it's Aunt Paulina's way of squeezing my heart from the outside. Punishment for my Thanksgiving performance is what she called it when she bawled me out for making her look like a fool in front of the Rathburn sisters. She's given up trying to get me to call her Mother, and I'm willing to pay any price to stand fast on that one. But she must be able to see it in my eyes—the fact that I'm not as cocky about living in a foster home as I was at first. You know how they say thinking you can do something and doing it are two different things? Well, it's true. The anger in Isaac's eyes makes me realize that I'd agree to just about anything to escape that fate. So when Aunt Paulina said that's where I'd end up if I didn't cut my hair, I wasn't about to take a chance that she'd back off again. Mama used to say, "Better the devil you know than the one you don't." I'm taking her advice on this one. Besides, I still haven't thought of a way to make her pay for killing my mother.

"I do want it short," I say, running a raggedy hangnail along the light green cape that's tied around my neck. I actually enjoy the sharp pain that zings through me when it gets caught in the fabric. Then I look directly at Helen and smile as convincingly as I can. "Most of my girl-friends have short hair and they love it. I'm just a little nervous is all. I've never been to a salon before."

Helen swallows hard but doesn't say anything. She checks the clasp of the Christmas tree pin that's attached to her collar. So many of the jewel ornaments have fallen off, the empty spots remind me of missing teeth, and I think, *What is the point of that?* Then she narrows her eyes and puckers her face as if she can smell a rat but isn't sure where it's hiding. She points the scissors at Aunt Paulina. "All right, Miss Hanson, I'll do it, but *you* have to make the first cut. So if she changes her mind, she can't blame me."

"Nobody's going to blame anybody, Helen," Aunt Paulina snaps, grabbing the scissors. She rests them on the nape of my neck, sending a cold zap of electricity down my back. Then color seeps into her face. "Jesus! You'd think we were about to cut her head off."

I'm used to hearing her swear at Nettie and me, so I don't think anything of it. But a tiny gasp escapes Helen's mouth that sounds as if she's been stabbed in the heart. She could pass for a preacher's wife—strict hair and no makeup. And I bet she drives an ugly-color sedan. The look she gives Aunt Paulina makes me think she's waiting for her to spit on the floor, then light up a cigarette and order a beer. "Miss Hanson, are you feeling all right?" she says with genuine concern in her voice. "You're not yourself today. I've never heard you talk like that."

"I'm fine, Helen," Aunt Paulina says in a condescending tone. "I'm just a little tired. I'm not used to raising a thirteen-year-old. I'm sorry I was short with you. I don't even know where that came from."

"That's all right." Helen sniffs and clears her throat. "We all get a little out of sorts once in a while. And I know what you mean about teenagers. My sister has one, and she's ready to tear her hair out."

As Helen walks over to the radio to turn down the volume on "Jingle Bells," Aunt Paulina grabs a handful of hair and twists hard, as if she's wishing it were my neck. I can see the satisfaction in her eyes as she looks at me in the mirror. She's about to get me good.

The scissors make a loud crunching sound. The blood is drumming through my head, and I feel as if I'm being smothered because I let all my air out and now I can't breathe in. As I look at the pile of hair on the floor, the memory of how Mama used to brush it every night tries to force its way into my brain, but I push it back out. There's no way I'm going to let Aunt Paulina know she's made me cry.

"Here you go, Helen," Aunt Paulina says, handing over the scissors. "Finish it up, but step on it. It's almost noon. My Christmas party for the underprivileged children is tomorrow, and I still have to order the refreshments."

"That's a wonderful thing you do, Miss Hanson," Helen says, like she's talking to Mother Teresa. "Those kids would have an awful bleak holiday if it wasn't for you. Your picture'll be in the paper again this year. I'll watch for it and save it for you." Then she turns to me and starts slicing away at my hair. "You're a lucky girl to be living with this saint of a woman. But I'm sure you already know that. You seem like a real nice kid."

"Well, what do you think?" Helen says, brushing the hair off the back of my neck with a towel. "Your aunt was right. I think you look just cunning, like a cute little pixie."

I stare at myself in the mirror and can't believe what's just happened. I hate Aunt Paulina. And I hate Helen for going along with her. I even hate Mama a tiny bit because she's supposed to be here so things like this don't happen.

"Katherine, Helen asked you a question," Aunt Paulina says in a singsong tone. She's standing next to me, putting on her coat. "She wants to know what you think about your new haircut."

I look straight at her and smile. "It looks nice."

Eleven

NETTIE'S DRIVING Aunt Paulina to the American Legion Hall. I lied and said I had an upset stomach when Aunt Paulina told me I had to help with the party. It would be fun to see the little kids. But I know Isaac is looking forward to this, and it would ruin it for him if I was there, watching him eat handout food and open charity gifts.

Aunt Paulina stayed away from the whiskey last night, and Nettie's tiptoeing around her foul mood. The car is so loaded with presents that there's hardly any place for Aunt Paulina to sit. I'm wondering why she didn't just have the man who delivered them to her house take them directly to the party. But then I remember Isaac saying how much she enjoys watching the kids' faces as she brings in their gifts. "Last year she even got down on the floor with the littlest ones and played with them while the photographer took her picture," he said. Now, that's something I'd love to see—Aunt Paulina crawling around on the floor in her black silk suit with a bunch of sticky-faced kids.

I watch the car disappear in the distance, and then I head upstairs to do what I've been planning since I moved here: snoop my brains out. This is the first time I've had the house to myself, and I'm not about to waste the opportunity. Even though Aunt Paulina told me to go right to bed and stay there until she gets back, I head straight for Mama's room. It's amazing the pull a place has on you when you've been warned a thousand times to keep out.

Nettie keeps the upstairs keys on a hook in the linen closet behind the towels and the extra bars of lilac-scented soap Aunt Paulina stores up like a pack rat, as if she's afraid the Yardley people will turn on her and cut off her supply. Aunt Paulina has the keys tagged and marked with her tight, perfect handwriting—no squiggles or curls.

As I'm turning the key in the lock, Mama's description of the room races through my head. There are a million things I want to see. First I'll go to the cubbyhole in the back of the closet, get her scrapbook and diary, and hide them in my room for later so I can read them in peace. Then I'll spend the rest of my time lying on her bed, browsing through her books and all the other things she told me about.

It feels strange to have to sneak around to look at something that should rightly be mine, and I think how Aunt Paulina approached this all wrong. When you get spoken to gently, you pay attention—a scream sends you scrambling for cover. And when you get something shoved down your throat, all you want to do is run away from the one who's doing the shoving. But then, even if she had gone about it the right way—kind and patient— she still wouldn't have gotten what she wanted: a girl who would love her.

When I open the door, a sound like a pigeon's call jumps out of my mouth and echoes back at me from the stark white walls. There's nothing here—not even a curtain at the window to interrupt the bleakness of it all. It's as if Mama's memory has been washed away completely, and the awful sight of it makes me feel as empty as the room.

My shoes make sharp, clicking noises on the hardwood floor where Mama's lavender carpet is supposed to be. The closet is open and the door to the tiny crawl space in the back is hanging on one hinge, guarding nothing. When I kneel down to see if maybe the diary and scrapbook have been overlooked, a loose corner of the bland milk-colored wallpaper catches my eye. I peel it back and discover one of Mama's lilies buried alive in a shallow grave.

At first, I aim my anger at Aunt Paulina. But then I realize it could have been Mama's parents who pulled her out by the roots and tossed her in the trash. How is it that a person can try to live her life the way people expect her to, and then one day a mistake can erase their love completely?

Aunt Paulina's room is what I expected—satiny and expensive—everything deep rose. Her trademark scent of Shalimar slinks around like a ghost, as if she's about to jump out from where she's hiding and put me in my place.

I'm trying to decide what to look at first when my father catches my eye. His photograph is on the nightstand, surrounded by smooth brown wood, and he's looking directly at me. When I pick up the frame and tilt it toward the window, I see a smudge of lipstick that hasn't been completely wiped away from the glass over his mouth. I've never seen this picture of him before, and there's a joy on his face that doesn't match my memory of him. He looks about seventeen, and his transparent blue eyes hold me captive.

Then a black cloud rolls over my mood, and I think how wild those eyes looked the night my daddy died.

Mama's lip was split deep and oozing blood, because she made the mistake of asking him if he'd clean the fish while she peeled the potatoes and got the rest of the supper under way. She was sorry, but the grocery store where she worked was having a sale and she had to stay late. He was in a good mood, so she took a chance and stepped over the danger line.

God wrapped my daddy in the wrong package. He was like a rat trap done up in pretty paper and finished off with a fancy bow. Mama'd opened that package enough times to know that mostly she'd get her hand snapped off, but the trimmings were more than she could resist. And every now and then, he'd give her what she wanted. Just often enough to keep the bait fresh.

This time, though, the smile dropped off his face, and he glared at her like he'd as soon kill her right there as look at her. Then he grabbed the fish bucket out of the sink, dumped the whole mess on her new white table-cloth, and said, "The least you can do is clean the god-damn fish. I spent the entire afternoon on the lake in the bitching cold. Christ Almighty! What more do you want from me?" That's when he punched her.

I wanted to scream that he was the one who had called in sick to work so he could go ice fishing with his buddies— sit in a warm shanty and drink beer. But I did what I always did. I kept my mouth shut so he wouldn't turn on me.

He told her he was going out for cigarettes and that supper'd better be ready when he got back. Then he slammed the kitchen door, and I heard his car race down the driveway.

WHEN THE DOORBELL rang, Mama asked me to answer it. "It's probably the paperboy," she said. "His money's on the TV. Then you can go wash up. Your father'll be home soon."

When I opened the door, two police officers were standing there with their hats in their hands and sadness in their eyes. And I knew. If I called for my mother like they wanted me to, it would have been the same as killing her, because no matter what she did, she'd never be able to get him to love her now. Instead, I stood there and wondered if I were dreaming the whole thing, because the inside of my head had gone black. As the officers walked past me, the smell of the perch Mama was frying—my favorite food in the whole world—turned my stomach, filling my mouth with thin, acidy spit, and I choked down the urge to throw up.

"A drunk driver ran a red light," I heard the older policeman say as I walked into the kitchen. "Your husband didn't have a chance."

Mama's face was so swollen, she didn't even look like herself. But she had my mother's apron on, and she was holding my mother's paring knife in one hand and a tomato in the other. When the officer's words reached her brain, the tomato dropped to the floor in slow motion and she squeezed the knife so tightly that drops of blood fell from her fingers onto the green linoleum.

I SIT ON Aunt Paulina's bed and use my sleeve to wipe her lipstick off my father's picture. It doesn't belong there. My mother should have had that happy man in the photograph, and it should have been her lipstick. I look at his face again and think how he used to call me Baby Kate when I was in the early grades at school, before he started drinking so much and didn't care anymore. Maybe if I could have stayed little and reminded him less of Mama, it would have been enough to keep him sober. But then I wipe my cheeks with the back of my hand, and anger replaces the sadness. He should have tried harder. He was lucky to have a wife like Mama who would do anything in the world for him. And a girl who would have loved him so big if he'd just given her the chance.

I put the photograph back on the nightstand and open the top drawer. When I see the scrapbook, my thoughts take a wrong turn. But then I see Aunt Paulina's name written on the cover—not Mama's. I open it and there's my father again, all dressed up in prom clothes with a flower in his lapel—a sweetheart rose, pale yellow. And standing next to him is Aunt Paulina, wearing a soft, light-colored dress with a flowing, uneven hem. And there's a rose corsage pinned to her waist with a sprig of baby's breath to finish it off. Her face is fresh and innocent, and my father is gazing down at her with a look on his face that I've never seen before—love, maybe.

I hold the book up to get a closer look and a stack of letters tied with a pink satin ribbon falls onto the bedspread. When I untie the bow, I recognize my father's writing on the envelopes—left handed, slanted the wrong way. A voice from inside me whispers in my ear not to open them, but I tell it to mind its own business.

As I read the sweet words that flowed from my father's heart onto the pages with a tenderness I never thought he was capable of feeling, my heart tightens and I wonder why he didn't show this gentle side to Mama. But why did he stay? He used to threaten all the time that he was going to go away and never come back. So maybe he *did* care for her. Not with the fierceness he loved Aunt Paulina, but in a lopsided, loyal way that kept him from leaving. And if he had married Aunt Paulina, would she have been the one with the smashed-up face?

It scares me when I think that maybe there's only one true love for each of us. I wonder where Mama's ended up. Dead, too, I hope, so nobody else can have him.

My eyes sting and I lick salty tears off my lips while I'm reading the letter he wrote to Aunt Paulina the day before he married Mama, the one where he tells her she won't be hearing from him again. I guess everybody has goodness in them, even though sometimes it's just a tiny speck that hardly shows. I wish my daddy hadn't had that tiny speck, though, because it was so much easier to hate him straight-out than to deal with the confusion that is whirling around in my head.

Twelve

I HAVE TO SPEND Christmas alone with Aunt Paulina. She insisted that Nettie take the day off. And I think that Nettie knew how hard Christmas would be for me without Mama, so she offered to come and make a nice dinner. But Aunt Paulina said no, that she wanted the whole day with just me. I am *not* looking forward to this. And I hate the thought of Nettie spending Christmas all by herself. She's the closest thing I have to a mother now, and I wish we could go somewhere together and leave Aunt Paulina home alone. Maybe if I pretend this is just a regular day, the ugliness of the whole thing will disappear.

I'm in the kitchen looking for the cornflakes when

Aunt Paulina comes in and announces that she's going to make us breakfast.

"Waffles or pancakes?" she says all bouncy, like she does this kind of thing every day.

I wait for her to tell me the real reason she's here, but when she repeats the question, I back up and say, "Pancakes, please."

You know how dogs are supposed to be able to smell danger? Well, my senses are on high alert. This is the kind of situation where you say to yourself: *Watch out! Whatever's coming isn't going to be good.*

"Katherine, why don't you go upstairs and get dressed," she says, pushing up her sleeves, then reaching for Nettie's apron on the hook behind the door. "I want you to look nice when you open your presents, so I can take your picture. I think you're going to like what I got you."

I stand on the rim of this curious mystery, unable to pull my feet from the muck of confusion so I can escape. This is the first time she's mentioned the mountain of presents under the tree with my name on them. I'm not sure how to feel. Part of me is dying to open them. The rest knows there'll be strings attached. I think I'll just pretend they're from Mama.

She looks up from the package of bacon she's taking from the refrigerator. "Well, don't just stand there," she chirps. "It's Christmas. Let's enjoy it."

It's spooky the way Aunt Paulina can be miserable one

minute and sweet the next. I get edgy when things don't stay in the right box, and it chokes me up good inside, like somebody has knocked all the wind out.

When I come back downstairs, still feeling jittery, Aunt Paulina says, "Syrup or raspberry jelly?" in her high-stepping voice. She's sitting next to me at the kitchen table, holding up a fancy container of real maple syrup, not the fake Log Cabin kind. Having her there has pushed the off button on my appetite, so I don't want either one. I love bacon and it's been a long time since I've had any, but I'm staring at the slices on my plate and wondering how I'm going to manage to get them down. The fat is still white— soft and shiny. She has to be the worst cook in the entire world.

"Well, which one?" she says in a teasing way like a cat rubbing its head against my knee. She's sitting sideways on her chair, and her crossed leg is swinging to the beat of the impatience in her head.

"Syrup, please," I say in a library voice, keeping my eyes on the mound of overdone pancakes on my plate.

"Pardon me?" She thrusts her head in my direction and cups her hand around her ear like an old person—the actress in her.

I know she heard me. I lift my chin, turn up the volume on my voice, and say, "I'd like syrup, please."

"Your mother used to love maple syrup," she says with softness in her tone.

This catches me off guard, and I let the shield drop away from my heart. "Even when she was a little girl?" The excitement in my voice gives me away and opens the door for her to come in.

"*Especially* when she was a little girl," she says, drumming the table with her fingertips. "Mother had to hide the bottle on the top shelf because Mimi would drink it down like water if she could get to it."

I've never heard my mother called Mimi before. She was always just Amy, even to my father. It startles me to hear her called a different name—an endearing nickname—from the wrong person.

She's not touching her food, and her knee is tapping against the edge of the table like a woodpecker gone crazy. Finally, she walks over to the counter, takes a whiskey bottle from the cupboard, and half fills a water glass. As she looks over at me, her chest rises and she blows heavy breath out her nose. Then she fills the glass the rest of the way and returns to her chair—no shame at all.

Good, this I can handle. She won't be able to stop. She'll lose interest in me and go upstairs. *Take a nice big drink,* I say to her in my head. And she does.

"OPEN THIS ONE first," Aunt Paulina says, handing me a present wrapped in thick gold paper with a matching wide ribbon hand-tied in a bow. She's sitting in a rose wing chair next to the Scotch pine she had flocked white and decorated at the florist's. Her glass is on the end table, nearly empty. I'm sitting on the carpet at her feet, the perfect place for opening presents, she said.

My grown-up self knows that this gift is a snake in disguise and I should hand it right back to her with a polite *no thank you*. But the little girl who still lives inside me—the one who has never even dreamed of having something this beautiful given to her for her very own, says, *Oh, no, you don't. It's yours to keep. It even has your name on it.*

"Go ahead, open it," she says, like she's got me now.

But the little girl ignores her tone. And before my heart completes a beat, I am holding up a raspberry cashmere sweater. SAKS the label says. FIFTH AVENUE.

After the dark blue skirt to complete the outfit comes a whole pile of clothes, including a coat, shoes, and even underwear. Then a jewelry box, a silver necklace, and a cute little radio.

For the grand finale, Aunt Paulina hands me the two small packages she's been holding on her lap the whole time—a birthstone ring and a gold bangle bracelet, fourteen carat.

"Well, do you like them?" she asks. She's refilled her glass and it's already half gone.

"Everything's beautiful," I say, so overwhelmed with my good fortune, I can hardly breathe.

She doesn't say anything, just looks at me with a calm face. I bet she thinks this is going to make up for what she did to Mama.

I remember the gift I bought for her and wrapped at Beamer's—reused paper from last year—with no bow and a homemade tag cut from the wrapping. After I saw all my presents, I knew I had to get her something. I lie on my stomach and reach to the back of the tree. "It's not much," I say, as I'm handing it to her. A week's pay from Mr. Beck—money I'd been saving for new shoes, but what does that matter now?

She unwraps the gift and takes another drink. Her eyes have welled up, and I don't know where to look. I stare at my hands and wait.

"It's lovely," she says, meaning it. "How did you know I was nearly out of Shalimar?"

"Just lucky, I guess." She's lying about being out because when I was in her room, besides the bottle on her dressing table, I saw an unopened box on the shelf in her bathroom with the cellophane still on it. But I didn't know what else to get her that would be safe. I always used to make Mama's gifts—from the heart is always better, she'd say. I don't think "from the heart" would cut it with Aunt Paulina. Besides, none of my heart will ever belong to her.

She cradles her drink with both hands and looks at me with contented eyes. Then she reaches out and touches my shoulder lightly. "I'm so glad you changed your mind."

I don't pull back like I want to. "Changed my mind about what?"

"About being my daughter," she says, as if I already knew what she meant.

I don't know what she's talking about. I don't say anything.

She takes a deep breath. "I know you never would have accepted my gifts if you hadn't."

Well, there it is. I should have known. Somebody's twisting a rubber band inside my head, but I keep my face regular and don't argue with her. I've never crossed her when she's been really drunk before, and I don't know what she would do. I wish Nettie were here.

She takes another long drink. "You were supposed to be mine, you know." She lays her head on the back of the chair and stares at the ceiling. "We even had a name picked out for you."

I know this part. In my father's letters to Aunt Paulina, the early ones, he talked about baby Natalie and baby Stevie and what a good mother he thought Aunt Paulina would be. And how they only had to wait another year before they could get married and start a family—as soon as Aunt Paulina finished secretarial school and he got moved up to supervisor at the paper mill.

"She ruined everything," she says, her voice cracking. Tears now. First one, then a river. She doesn't bother to wipe them away. It's as if she's alone, talking to herself. "We all spoiled her because she was plain and gawky and we felt sorry for her. She was used to getting everything she wanted. And if she didn't get it, she took it."

I'm wondering how you can take a person if he doesn't want to go.

"Lily was engaged, and Mimi didn't have anybody. I asked Jake to take her places and do things with her so she wouldn't be alone while I was away at school."

Mama called Daddy "Jacob," an old person's name, like he was her father. Jake sounds like a boyfriend that you could laugh and have fun with.

She tips the empty glass to her lips, frowns, then puts it on the end table. "How was I to know she'd set a trap? She always acted like a child when he was around, as if he were her big brother." There's no expression in her voice, just straight-line words. "He said he was willing to wait until we were married so our wedding night would be special, but Mimi put an end to *that* dream."

The letter with the tearstains and the smudged ink told about the night he'd taken Mama to the movies and then for an ice-cream cone. She wanted to walk the long way home because it was warm out and they could wade in the river. Once they were there, the river wasn't enough for her. He was so sorry. It didn't mean anything to him. And all the other times didn't mean anything, either; they just happened. He hoped she could forgive him, but Mama was in trouble and it was his fault for being weak and he had to do right by her. That was one thing his mother had drummed into his head: you take responsibility for your actions, no matter what. He'd never stop loving Aunt Paulina as long as he lived. He hoped knowing that would make her feel better.

An awkward silence goes on forever, and I'm wondering if she's thinking what I'm thinking. He could have said no.

AUNT PAULINA'S taking a nap, and I'm trying on my new clothes and listening to the radio—Christmas carols because that's all I can find. I'm looking at my reflection in the mirror and thinking how good I look. It's amazing how special expensive clothes can make you feel. I've had nice things before, but they've always had somebody else's name on them—creases from the real owner's arms in the sleeves, a stain from a meal in a fancy restaurant, or maybe a whisper from the person who smoked cigars in the house where the other girl lived. This time there are just a few fold wrinkles and a memory of the scent the saleswoman was wearing when she slid everything into soft nests of tissue paper and then sent the gift-wrapped boxes through the mail to their lucky new owner.

I think how much fun it'll be to go back to school with a whole new wardrobe. I'll make Ashleigh Parke and her stuck-up cronies look like weeds. But then I think about Miss Plain and it kills the spirit of my good mood, because if you don't count the way they look, she and Mama were cut out of the same piece of soft cloth. And about an hour ago, I betrayed my mother in the worst possible way. I kept quiet and let Aunt Paulina think I was going to call her Mother. I wanted these things so badly. And it was the only way she'd stop crying. Plus, she was drunk, so she probably won't even remember. But *I* will. I picture Mama looking down and seeing what I've done, and I feel ashamed. You can't hide from your conscience for long. It finds you and bites—hard.

I tuck the gifts safely back into their boxes, and as I'm leaving them outside Aunt Paulina's room, I hear music through the door—Hank Williams singing "Your Cheatin' Heart." I'm surprised, but on the way back to my room, I remember when I was little and Daddy wasn't drinking, he used to joke around about wanting to be Hank Williams when he grew up. He'd sit Mama and me down on the couch and sing "Cold, Cold Heart" or "Lovesick Blues" while we hummed backup harmony. It was times like those that would trick us into thinking he was going to keep his promise to stop hurting Mama. I guess my father sang those songs to Aunt Paulina, too.

I'm looking out my window at the Becks' house when

I remember the gift Nettie told me she left in my dresser drawer. This one is wrapped in a white lace hanky tied up with a thin red ribbon. When I open it, the gold cross on a chain that I've seen around Nettie's neck since I got here falls onto my bed. Why would she give me something so personal? She asks me every week to go to church with her and I always refuse. Maybe this is just another nudge. Then I notice that my initials are embroidered on the hanky—even the *J* for my middle name, Jeannette. The stitches are loose and crooked like the ones on her apron. I wonder how she knows my whole name. A shuddery feeling runs through me when I remember that Mama said I was named for my grandmothers. Her mother was Katherine, and she told me so much about her, I felt as if I knew her. But my father's mother was a mystery. The one time I asked where she was, Daddy's face bristled the way the hackles rise on a dog's back and I left it alone. It's cold in this room, so I don't know why I'm sweating.

I never thought about Nettie being a nickname for anything. Besides, it could be short for names other than Jeannette—Annette or Antoinette, even Henrietta. That's all there is to it. There's nothing more to think about. Plus, this is stupid. She would have just told me. And she doesn't look anything like my father.

But then I remember what Mr. Beck said about going

home to my grandmother and how Nettie knew about my birthday. But she *can't* be my grandmother. My father's mother has to be dead and buried. No live mother would let her son grow up in a place that would kill his soul and make him mean. I shove the necklace back into the hanky and hide it under the things in my nightstand drawer.

I have to get away from all of this. Plus, I don't want to be here when Aunt Paulina sees that I've returned her gifts. The last time I was at their house, Mr. Talson invited me over for the day if I didn't have anything else to do. But Weesie'll be there and Mrs. Talson. You have to be in just the right mood for that. So before I know how I got here, I find myself knocking on Mr. Beck's front door. I'm not even wearing a coat.

"I'M SO GLAD you came over, Katherine," Mr. Beck says, looking at the plate of spaghetti in front of me. "If you hadn't, we'd be eating ham-and-cheese sandwiches instead of this feast you made."

I glance at the Ragu jar on the counter. "It wasn't any trouble," I say. "And I know how much Johnny loves spaghetti."

"Well, dig in, then," Mr. Beck says. "We don't stand on ceremony here." His eyes are vacant for a second and I'm just guessing, but I think he might have gone back to a time when Mrs. Beck was alive and Christmas dinner was served with lots of ceremony, in the dining room by the maids I heard so much about: him carving the roast goose with chestnut stuffing and Mrs. Beck passing the ambrosia salad in a cut-glass bowl. Today he struggles to tuck his paper napkin into the neck of his shirt before he picks up the big plastic fork that's equipped with a special finger grip so he can feed himself.

He's right across from me, and I'm not sure where to look. Until today I've only seen him drink coffee. With that, he waits until it's cool. Then he uses both hands to pick it up. He must sense my uneasiness, because he holds up the fork and says, "Quite a thing, isn't it?"

I nod.

Then he adds, "The old-people experts have thought of everything. I even have a gadget I use to put on my socks. And another one that helps me pick up things."

Johnny stops eating, reaches over, and pinches his grandfather's arm. "Yeah . . . the good old lobster claw." This is the first thing he's said since I came. When I asked him what he got for Christmas, he ran to his room and stayed there until Mr. Beck called him for dinner. Now he's sitting next to me, wearing a new winter jacket, leather gloves, and a cardboard magician's hat. He spread his other presents on the floor by my chair—the rest of the magic set, a gyroscope, and a checkers game.

"Johnny got quite a haul," I say to Mr. Beck. I know if I mention the gifts to Johnny, he'll bolt again.

"Lily sent the clothes," he says. A tiny look of sadness crosses his face. "I was hoping she'd be able to get home, but she's gone to Europe with a French horn player she met in a fish market, of all places. And, well . . . Santa brought the rest."

"Oh, nice" is the lame reply that decides to come out of my mouth.

"And what did you get?" Mr. Beck asks. He's back to his upbeat self.

"My aunt gave me lots of clothes and jewelry." I try to smile so it looks real.

"And what about your grandmother? I know she wouldn't forget you."

Well, there it is. It couldn't be any plainer than that. I was enjoying the spaghetti so much. Now my stomach is all tightened up, and I can't eat another bite. I have a terrible feeling about this. It reminds me of how Mama gave me hints when she got sick, before she told me outright that she was going to die. When you are given pieces of a puzzle a little at a time, the final picture isn't usually very pretty. "She gave me a beautiful gold necklace," I say. I don't even try to sound excited. And it's not one bit beautiful. The cross is all banged up, and most of the gold is worn off the chain.

"Well," he says, "it sounds as if Santa was good to both of you."

A huge smile covers Johnny's face. "Yeah," he says. "Santa's a good old guy."

After dinner Johnny goes up to his room. Mr. Beck doesn't make a move to get up, so I stay with him. I think he's as lonely as I am, and I'd rather be here than anywhere else.

For a minute we just sit, but then he says, "So what's Paulina up to?"

"Nothing," I say. "She's taking a nap."

He smiles. "Well, that's always fun." Then his face turns serious. "How are you two getting along?"

"Okay," I lie.

He must know what I'm thinking, because he says, "I can imagine how difficult this must be for you. She's not exactly the motherly type."

All I do is shake my head.

He reaches over and puts his hand on mine. "Your mother wrote me a letter before she died."

"Really?" She never said anything about it to me.

"She told me you knew everything that happened between her and Paulina."

I nod. "I do."

"Poor little Amy," he says with sadness in his voice. "Paulina did everything she could think of to torture her."

I have no idea what he's talking about. "I know."

"Amy just stood there and pretended it didn't bother her every time Paulina told her she was ugly and that no man would ever want her. I think that's why Amy did what she did, to prove her sister wrong."

So that's what happened. I keep nodding, hoping he won't stop talking. "I think so, too." I wonder why Mama never mentioned how mean Aunt Paulina was to her. Maybe she believed all that stuff. And I bet that's why she never stood up to Daddy.

Mr. Beck shakes his head just a little and lets out the breath he's been holding. "Paulina's just like her father," he says. "I don't think she'll ever let go of the past, and it's eating her alive, so things might not get much better."

I had that pretty much figured out. "I know."

"Your mother was worried about what it would be like so she wrote to ask me a favor."

"A favor?" This house is so big. Maybe he's going to say I can live here.

"Just to keep an eye out for you and make sure you're all right."

Oh. "That's nice of you."

"You're welcome to come over any time, Katherine. And if there's ever anything I can do for you, just ask."

"I will. Thank you."

Now we're sitting here not saying anything. Maybe I should get up and start the dishes.

"I wish you could meet Lily." He's staring at me with empty eyes.

"I wish I could, too," I say. I try to sound enthused about it because I know how much it would mean to him to have her come home.

"When Johnny was born," he says in a low voice, "we knew he'd never be normal. Lily just couldn't handle it, so she left and hasn't come back."

He looks so unhappy. I have to say something. "She'll probably come home real soon. Maybe she's just been too busy." Well, that was dumb. "I bet she'll come home any day now."

"I doubt it," he says. "But I keep her room the same as she left it, just in case."

I wonder how she can do that, just go away and leave her family and not come back.

Mr. Beck must have read my thoughts the way Mrs. McGillveray used to read tea leaves, because he says, "It's not always what you've lost that makes you sad. Sometimes it's what you have that breaks your heart."

I can't think of anything to say back, so I smile and start stacking the dishes. Mr. Beck follows me to the sink. "You shouldn't have to work on Christmas, Katherine," he says, as I'm squirting Dawn into the sink and swishing the water around to make suds. "Just put the plates on the counter, and I'll dry them the best I can."

I think he's trying to keep busy the same as I am so this desolate day will go by faster. I slow down my part of the job so he can do his. While I'm stalling, the thought of Nettie's necklace returns to my head.

"I didn't know until today that Nettie's my grandmother." I say it right out loud before I have time to think about it.

He looks at me, startled. "You didn't? She hasn't told you yet?"

"No."

"And your mother never mentioned her?"

"No, never."

"What about your father? He didn't tell you anything about his mother?"

"Nothing. I thought she was dead."

"Oh," he says, flabbergasted. "I assumed you knew."

I can tell he isn't just talking about Nettie being my grandmother. It's a whole lot more than that.

"Why did they keep her a secret?" I ask. I start washing a glass and try to act casual. Maybe he'll tell me if I don't seem all nuts about it.

Only silence from him.

"Mr. Beck?"

He shrugs his shoulders and turns his hands palm-side

out. "She'll have to tell you that herself. It isn't my place. I should never have said anything." He makes a *tsk* sound with his tongue. "I just thought you knew."

I stop washing and look over at him.

He must see the disappointment and confusion in my eyes. He puts his hand on my shoulder and says, "She's a good woman, Katherine. And I'm sure she loves you more than anything or she wouldn't be there." He gives me his sweet, knowing smile. "Just let her tell you in her own good time."

"Where were you?" Aunt Paulina's standing in the up-stairs hall. "It's late. I was worried." The smell of whiskey is strong, and her words come out with no expression at all. She's holding the bottle of Shalimar I gave her. There's still a bit of wrapping paper attached to it.

"I went to see Mr. Beck and Johnny. I wanted to wish them a merry Christmas. I didn't mean to be gone so long." I try to get by her, but she moves and blocks my way. This is the first time I've seen her without makeup and she looks plain—old, even.

"Was there something wrong with the gifts I gave you? I thought you liked them." There's sarcasm in her voice now.

"They're nice," I say. "I just can't keep them."

"Why not?"

"Because you want too much. You want a daughter and I'll never be that."

She reaches out to stroke my face but loses her balance and falls against the wall instead. "Why do you have to make this so hard?"

"You killed my mother." The words march out of my mouth on their own—single file and powerful.

Her jaw drops opens, but nothing comes out. Then she holds up the perfume, and at first I think she's going to hit me with it. Instead, she hands it to me and goes into her room. As I'm walking down the hall, I hear loud sobbing.

When I get to my room, I drop the perfume into the wastebasket. Then, without getting undressed, I crawl into bed and bury my head in the pillow so nobody can hear me cry.

Thirteen

"YOUR HOUSEKEEPER'S your grandmother?" Beamer asks. "How come you didn't know that?"

"Because nobody told me."

"Then how can you be sure?"

I tell her about the necklace and what Mr. Beck said.

"Why don't you tell her you know and ask her why it's such a deep, dark, scary secret?"

"I almost did when I thanked her for the necklace, but I chickened out. Then every night at supper, I try, but I just can't."

"Why not?"

"I don't know. I guess I'm afraid of what I'll find out. Like maybe I'm better off not knowing."

"Well, how bad can it be?" she says. "I mean it's not like she's a criminal or something. Maybe she's just embarrassed about being a maid."

"Yeah," I say. "That's probably it." That's not it. It's a lot worse than that. And since I found out who she is, I've wanted so many times to come right out with it and get it over. But then I remember what Mr. Beck said about waiting for her to be the one to bring it up. Part of me wants to tell her how thrilled I am to have a grandmother who loves me and works so hard to make everything just right. But there's another part of me—the angry part that wonders where she's been all my life and where she was when my father was growing up. Mothers don't just abandon their little boys and let them grow up with strangers. And grandmothers don't ignore baby granddaughters.

Beamer, Weesie, and I are on our way to Isaac's house to see if he wants to go to skating at the community park. We called his number, but a little kid answered and all he kept saying was no. So we decided it would be easier to go get him.

"Are you sure he's not your boyfriend?" Weesie asks Beamer for the millionth time.

"I'm *sure*," Beamer says. "He's just a friend. Now stop bugging me about it or I'll take you back home and leave you there."

"You can't leave me there," Weesie says. "Mommy said you have to babysit the whole day. Later on we can play with my new Barbies. You'll be Ken. And Kat can be Skipper. And I think this Isaac person really is your boyfriend. Excuse me. I need a cigarette." She skips ahead of us, holds her fingers to her lips, then watches her breath rise into the freezing air.

Beamer sighs and shakes her head. "This is going to be one long day."

I laugh at how funny Weesie looks. She's wearing a tutu over her snowsuit pants, and she has her new Christmas skates draped over her shoulder as if she's trying to look like a professional.

"THIS IS IT," Beamer says. "It's number twenty-five." We're in front of a neat yellow house with a wreath on the door and a plastic Santa near the front step. And you can see the outline of a Christmas tree through the picture window.

"I don't think so," I say. This can't be where Isaac lives. He's always talking about how horrible it is. It's probably the one next door with all the junk on the lawn. I turn toward the other house. "Let's try over there."

"Isaac told me he lives with the Raymonds," Beamer says. "There's only one Raymond in the book, and they live at twenty-five Hickory. This is twenty-five." She starts toward the door.

"*I* get to ring the bell," Weesie says, running ahead of Beamer.

I follow, still thinking this is the wrong house.

An old man answers the door. His clothes are rumpled, and I don't think he shaves every day. "Yeah?" is all he says. You can tell by his voice that we've disturbed him.

Weesie moves back beside Beamer and grabs my hand.

"We're looking for Isaac Harper," Beamer says. "Is this the right house?"

There's a baby standing next to the man now. She's about two years old. All she's wearing is a soggy diaper, no shirt. "That Isaac kid," the guy says, "he's not here anymore." The baby grabs hold of the man's shirttail. He swats her hand away. She whimpers, then sticks her thumb in her mouth. He starts to close the door.

"Wait!" Beamer says. "Where is he?"

"How should I know? They come. They go. It's not my job to keep track." He looks over at a girl about eight years old who's standing beside him now. The one who's been staring at Weesie with huge eyes since she came to the door. "Go get Mrs. Raymond," the man says to the girl. "And tell her to move it. I'm heating the whole outdoors."

"Hi, Barbara Ann," Weesie says.

The girl gives Weesie a shy smile and then she's gone.

As the man's closing the door, he says, "My wife'll be right here. She can tell you how to get in touch with that kid. She's in charge of all that stuff."

As soon as the door closes, Weesie says, "That's Barbara Ann Pietrek. She's in my class at school." Then in a low voice, "Some of the kids make fun of her because she wets her pants."

"You came to see Isaac?" The wife is standing at the door, holding a newborn baby and a letter. She's round and red faced and frazzled looking, but a little bit pretty, not as old as the husband.

Beamer looks hopeful, as if the man had it all wrong. "So he *does* still live here," she says.

The woman shakes her head. "The social worker picked him up on Christmas Eve. She said his father had straightened his life out and was getting him back."

"But don't they have to tell the person?" Beamer asks. "Can they just spring it on them like that?" Her voice has gone all high and squeaky.

"Well, he knew it was in the works. He just didn't know the exact date," the woman says. "I guess his father wanted to give him a Christmas surprise."

"But how come he . . . ?"

"Look, kids, I gotta go. Isaac's replacement's due any minute, so I have a ton of things to do." She starts to close the door, but then opens it again. She holds out the envelope and squints at the writing on the front. "Is anybody here Beamer?"

"That's me," Beamer says.

"Well, Isaac asked me to give you this if you came looking for him." She hands Beamer the envelope. "I guess he knew you would."

"Thanks," Beamer says. She holds the letter so tightly, you'd think the woman had just given her a hundred-dollar bill.

As we're turning to leave, Mrs. Raymond says, "He was a good kid. And I've never seen anybody that smart. He didn't do a minute of homework, and he still brought home straight A's." She stops a second to think about it, then nods her head. "Yup. You gotta be awful smart to do that."

I'M TRYING to keep Weesie occupied by making a miniature snowman while Beamer stands by the park gate, reading Isaac's letter. It's only one page, so she must have read it ten times by now.

"Come on, Bernadette," Weesie calls. "Let's go!"

Beamer puts the letter back, folds the envelope, and then zips it into her jacket pocket. "I'm coming," she says. "Don't be so impatient."

"You okay?" I ask.

She nods. "He's fine. His father got married again and bought a house in Boston. The new wife teaches at a college there." She shrugs. "I guess I should be happy for him." Her look has gone a little sad, so I think she's leaving out the part about how much she's going to miss him. And she must feel a little betrayed because he didn't tell her in person that he'd probably never see her again. Maybe it was easier for him to write it than say it straight-out.

"Put *my* skates on first," Weesie says. She's sitting on a bench next to the pond, taking off her boots.

"Okay," Beamer says, "but then you have to wait till we get ours on so we can hold you up. Now sit still so I can get these things laced."

Weesie crosses her arms and looks at Beamer with strict eyes. "But I already know how to skate."

"You don't know how to skate," Beamer says. "This is the first time you've even had them on."

"Well, I've watched the girls on TV and it looks pretty easy. I bet I can even do those jumps and twirls." She starts to get up.

Beamer pulls Weesie back down and looks at her with raised eyebrows. "You just sit there until Kat and I can help you, or I'll take those skates right back off."

I'm just as surprised as Weesie to hear Beamer talk like this. I wait for Weesie to throw a fit.

She looks at Beamer, then at me. She lifts her chin and speaks in her affected tone. "I'm a little tired. I think I'll just rest a minute before I start."

When Beamer and I have our skates on, she looks at Weesie. "Okay, then, I'll hold one of your hands and Kat'll hold the other." We pull her up. "Now just pretend you're walking so you can get the feel of the ice," Beamer says. "Got it?"

"Got it," Weesie says in an exasperated voice. "But I

want to go under that bridge like those big kids are doing."

"We'll go under the bridge another day. Today we're going to stay at this end where it's not crowded."

Weesie rolls her eyes at Beamer. "Yeah, right," she says, "the baby end."

Before we have a chance to take one step, Weesie pulls her hands out of her mittens and starts running toward the stone bridge in the middle of the pond. When she falls, there's pure silence for a second and then the screaming starts.

"Oh my god," Beamer says. "She must really be hurt. She never cries.

"WHAT'S THE *matter* with you? How could you let this happen?" Mrs. Talson's watching the emergency room doctor put a cast on Weesie's arm and yelling at Beamer at the same time. Her face looks as if it's about to explode.

"I didn't *let* it happen," Beamer says. "It just happened."

"But you have to watch her. She's little. You should have been more careful. You shouldn't have been doing something that dangerous."

"What are you talking about? You *knew* where we were going. You *told* me to take her."

"But I *thought* you'd be careful."

Beamer clamps her mouth shut and stares straight

ahead. Maybe she's counting to ten so she doesn't say something really sassy and get in more trouble.

"Well?" Mrs. Talson says. "What do you have to say for yourself?"

"Nothing. I have nothing to say to you."

Oh boy. She's going to get *killed*.

Mrs. Talson's mouth falls open, but only air comes out.

Beamer looks down at Weesie and her eyes start to overflow. She lays her head on the pillow and talks softly. "I'm sorry you got hurt."

"I know," Weesie says. "But the nurse gave me a little pink pill so now it doesn't hurt at all."

Beamer kisses Weesie's cheek.

"Bernadette?" Weesie says.

"What?"

"The next time we go, I'll stay at the baby end and walk like you told me to. I just wanted to see what real skating felt like. It doesn't feel so good."

The doctor chuckles. Mrs. Talson gives him a dirty look.

"I'm going now," Beamer tells Weesie. "When you get home, we can play Barbies. I'll be Ken."

"And Kat'll be Skipper?" Weesie says, looking over at me.

"Yeah. I'll be Skipper," I say. "I can't wait to be Skipper."

Fourteen

WE'RE SITTING at the dining-room table, and Mr. Beck is teaching me how to type. "You're doing just fine," he says all upbeat after I've hit another wrong key and bitten my lip so hard, I taste blood. "It takes awhile to get the hang of it." I bet inside he's begging God for patience and probably a big bottle of aspirin for the headache I've given him.

He's a stickler about not looking. He says the extra time it takes will be worth it in the long run. My brain is wringing its hands, and I'm thinking if he let me look, he might get his book typed before we're both dead and buried.

Johnny's sitting on the other side of Mr. Beck, eating a Sugar Daddy and sketching me on the back of a receipt of some kind he found in one of the piles of papers in the middle of the floor. A trickle of sugary spit is walking down his chin. Mr. Beck tried getting his attention by clearing his throat and wiping his own chin, but Johnny didn't get the hint, so Mr. Beck takes out his handkerchief. "Here, look at me a minute," he says to Johnny. "You've got just a little bit of a problem going on here." Johnny lifts his chin but keeps looking down and drawing while Mr. Beck wipes away the drool and then puts his handkerchief back in his pocket.

I think how brilliant Mr. Beck is and how he doesn't treat Johnny like he's broken, but as if he's exactly the grandson he wished for his entire life.

"Well, that's it for chapter one," Mr. Beck says in a cheery voice. "We'll do the revisions in pencil, and after we're done, we'll put it through the typewriter again." Then he looks at me as though I should be in a jewelry store window. "You did a great job, Katherine. You can't imagine what a big help this is. I'm beginning to feel as if I'm worth something again." A compliment straight-out. Now that's something a person doesn't get every day.

On the outside I fidget with my hands and I'm not sure what to say back, so I just sit here, smiling like a ninny. But inside I feel warm and cozy because of the praise he just gave me. And if I knew him well enough, I'd tell him he was worth a whole lot even before he started writing again.

"I'm going to try to get a nap in before dinner," Mr. Beck says, getting up from the table. The creaking complaints of his old bones come across the room loud and clear. Then he nearly trips over a pile of newspapers he didn't see. "One of these days I'll have to clean up this mess before somebody kills himself."

"*I'll* do it if you'd like," I say fast, hoping he'll say yes, because there are still a couple of hours before I go home, and Johnny rarely says a word while I'm here. He just follows me around, watches whatever I do, and pulls hairs out of his eyebrows so there's almost nothing left. I think I'm the cause of that, because when I first came, he had thick caterpillar eyebrows. Now it looks as though the caterpillars crawled off his face and left only stubbly trails.

"Do you really want to?" Mr. Beck sounds shocked, as though I'd just offered to carry him up the stairs.

"Sure, I like to put things in order." This is true about me. I am not fishing for brownie points. I like to tidy up and clean. I take after Mama in that respect. She used to say that when your soul is in shambles, you tend to work extra hard on the things you can control. And I've learned that when you are put together in a neat package on the outside and you keep your surroundings in a fastidious manner, people will think, *Well, she's just fine. There's nothing to pick apart here.* So they will move their gossipy selves to somebody else and leave you alone.

"All right, then," he says, walking toward me, working his mouth like he's adjusting something with his tongue—loose false teeth, I bet. "Why don't you start with the newspapers. You can sort them by year and put them in one big pile in the closet over there. I've been meaning to do that forever. I just never got around to it." He gives me an odd look—confusion, maybe. "I can't even remember why I saved most of them. As soon as the book is done, I'll go through them and we can cut out whatever I thought was important and then they can go to the dump."

"Oh, okay," I say. "That's a good idea." But I have a feeling that you-know-where will freeze over before he'll get to that job. A man who saves broken rubber bands and grocery lists from twenty years ago and stacks of magazines that he plans to finish reading when he has a minute isn't likely to send much to the dump.

JOHNNY'S SITTING next to me now. When he sees the photograph on the front page of the newspaper I got from the oldest-looking pile on the floor, he puts down his root beer and pulls the paper over to him. He slumps in his chair, and the sun sets on his face as he traces the handsome young sailor in the picture with his finger—lightly, as though he doesn't want to hurt him. He starts twisting the top button on his shirt. When it won't go any further, he gives it one last try, and it slips from his fingers and lands on the table. He scoops it up, pops it into his mouth, and sucks on it like it's a Life Saver. Then he fiddles with Mama's wedding ring. The day I asked him to give it back, his face clouded over. I felt mean because I really didn't want it. It just seemed wrong that he was wearing it as if we were going steady. But when a person like Johnny loves you, it's as pure as anything—not something to fool around with—so I told him he could keep it.

"That's my father," he says in his deep, slow-talking way. He looks into my eyes on purpose for the first time since I've known him, so I can see *his* eyes up close. They're a drab, medium brown, and for some strange reason, they remind me of the soft velvet of a puppy's ear. "He used to live on a big boat, but now he lives in heaven with God and Nana."

"This man is your father?" I ask. I think he's making up a story like he does when he comes in from the bus and tells his grandfather what he did in school, like putting out fires and saving his teacher from robbers.

He lowers his eyes, then leaps from his chair and runs toward the stairs. I'm used to this by now, so I don't think much of it. He'll hide in his room until I'm gone, and then tomorrow he'll be his regular straight-line self until I make a mistake and look at him wrong or say something that confuses him. I believe that when his brain has to work overtime, it's easier for him to go somewhere safe and quiet where he can think at his own speed.

I'm nearly finished reading the article below the sailor when Johnny comes back into the room, clutching something to his chest. It's white and at first I think it's another of his drawings that he will hand me without looking to see the surprised expression on my face. I have collected a whole shoe box of them, and they still astound me every time I look at them.

The photograph Johnny lays on the table is crackled and limp around the edges, as if it's been worn out by being looked at too much. The boy in the picture is the one from the newspaper—John Murdoch, Petty Officer Third Class. Only here he's in a T-shirt and jeans, still alive—the bombs haven't blown him to pieces yet—and he has his arm around Lily Beck and they're looking at each other with love on their faces. They're sitting on a blanket, having a picnic, toasting the camera with Cokes. Lily looks like Princess Grace—exactly the way Mama described her—and John Murdoch looks like Johnny Beck, only bright-eyed and confident.

"It's a nice picture, Johnny," I say, handing it back to him.

"Yeah," he says. "It's nice." And then he's gone.

I pick up another paper, thumb through it, and find Mrs. Beck's obituary. She was pretty, just like Mama said.

IT'S DARK when I head home. A million stars have burned bright, flickering holes in the black sky that goes on forever. It is deep winter—the middle of January—one of those days when it's so cold, it hurts your lungs to breathe and your feet squeal on the snow-covered sidewalk.

On my way up the driveway to the back door, I see the top half of Nettie's head through the kitchen window. Then steam fogs the glass and she's gone. She's probably draining potatoes in the sink, making sure supper will be ready when I get home like she does every night. She'll whip them with the electric mixer so no lumps are left, add just enough cream to make them fluffy, melt butter in the valley she'll press out with the bowl of a spoon, then watch my face to see if I approve.

She serves Aunt Paulina at the dining-room table— usually salmon steak or lamb chops with roasted baby potatoes and fresh asparagus. Sometimes a veal cutlet pounded thin with a special tomato sauce poured over the top—food she has Nettie buy just for her.

When Aunt Paulina's safely in her bedroom, Nettie and I eat together in the kitchen. It's fine with me because I'm not crazy about salmon, and eating baby animals is not something I could do with a clear conscience. If you don't count her oatmeal and mustard pickles, Nettie's a good cook. Last night we had fried bologna—the chunk kind you can cut nice and thick—and macaroni and cheese topped with buttery bread crumbs and a can of Libby peas. Then rice pudding with raisins for dessert.

While we're eating, she tells me stories about when she was a little girl, growing up in Canada. And I take in her words as fast as her cooking. I don't want to miss anything important like what she's doing here, working for Aunt Paulina. But she stays on the other side of the border where it's safe and dull. It must have been when she came to the States that the secret part of her life began.

I think of the article in Mr. Beck's *Brattleboro Gazette* and how my mouth dropped open when I saw Nettie's picture on the front page.

The date: a month to the day before Mama was buried.

The banner headline:

AREA WOMAN RELEASED FROM PRISON

The story began:

After serving twenty-five years of a life sentence for her husband's murder, Jeannette Farrington . . .

It felt as if somebody were pressing down hard on my chest.

> Attorney tried to prove self-defense . . . years of abuse . . . multiple broken bones . . . victim violated restraining order . . . three shots to the head.

The gasp I let out made Johnny look over, but since Nettie's picture was taken the day the trial ended, he must not have recognized her, so he went back to work.

> Young son taken to hospital on numerous occasions . . . broken arm . . . wrist . . . collarbone . . . ribs . . . victim never charged . . . child declared ward of the state . . . moved to an orphanage in a small town up north.

The fact that Johnny doesn't know how to read and wasn't looking anyway didn't keep me from protecting the words with my arm while I was studying the article.

> Time off for good behavior . . . model prisoner.

In my mind now is every Saturday afternoon when I thought Daddy was working overtime. Him driving two hundred miles, hoping the car wouldn't break down. Her in a drab gray prison dress, so happy to see him, asking a million questions about his job, his home, Mama, and me. Him with a thankful heart for what she did for him.

Even though I ask my brain not to fill in the blanks the article left out, it does anyway.

> Nobody saw him; it was her word against his. The little boy fell down a lot, what a pity! He always was

a clumsy child. And the wife instigated it, egged him on. Any red-blooded man would have reacted the same way.

I picture Nettie's nose, the crooked bump, and think how much that must have hurt. And I wonder if her eyes turned black like Mama's did.

The article shoves its fist in my face again:

She shot him in the back of the head after he'd put the gun on the table. He just wanted to talk, reason with her—*the prosecutor's trump card.* Life in prison. She's still a young woman. With good behavior, she'll be out in . . .

Tonight, the oh-so-good aroma of fried chicken greets me at the door. Nettie's standing at the stove, stirring flour into the pan drippings to make the milk gravy that I love so much. You have to be patient with this part and take enough time to loosen all the tasty brown bits from the bottom. Then stir fast when you add the milk so it will be smooth and just the right consistency. I watched Mama make it for as long as I can remember. I just never knew where the recipe came from.

I FINISH THE LAST of my apple cobbler, wipe my mouth with the daisy-covered napkin, and look Nettie straight in the eye. "It must have been terrible," I say. It's taken me all this time to find the courage to bring it up. But now that I know the truth, I have to let her know how I feel, because I don't think she could ever tell me.

She'd been going on about the time when she was a teenager and had spent the day in her neighbor's garden, picking butter beans, and how sunburned she'd got.

"Well, it wasn't terrible, but I didn't sleep very well that night." When she sees my face, her mouth turns down at the corners and settles into a crooked line. Then she lowers her eyes and fiddles with the handle of her coffee cup.

"I meant prison," I say, leaning toward her, trying to get her to look at me. The word *prison* tastes metallic in my mouth as pictures of iron bars and a cold, locked cell crawl into my mind. And the thought of Nettie spending all those years there makes a lump come into my throat that's so huge, I can't swallow.

"I know what you meant," she says, blinking once, then again. She presses her hands together, leans her elbows on the table, and rests her lips on the points of her fingers. "I just wasn't sure when you'd find out. I tried so many times to tell you, but I didn't know how." She takes a rumpled hanky from her apron pocket and wipes her dry nose. "I was afraid you'd hate me and I didn't want to lose you— you're all I have." She looks up and stares at me with solemn eyes. Her plastic glasses frames are old, faded to a pale orangey yellow. They sit crooked on her face—one thin, gray eyebrow showing more than the other.

"I just wish I had known," I say. "Daddy should have told me."

"I made him promise not to," she says in a defeated voice. "I had no idea you'd end up in Ellenville. I was hoping you'd grow up and move on to a faraway city and never have to know the truth. I tried to get him to leave Vermont, but he wouldn't. He wanted to be close to me so he could come visit. Imagine. He still loved me after all he'd been through. I thought he'd hate me for what I did."

"I wonder why Aunt Paulina didn't tell me," I say, thinking out loud. "It seems to me she would have loved to."

"I told her if she said anything that I would quit. I wouldn't have, but she didn't know that." A tiny laugh rolls out of her mouth. "Besides, she didn't want you to know any more than I did. She wanted you to think she was your only relative. She said if I told you, she'd fire me." She runs her finger across her lips, then drops her arm to the table. "I'm so sorry," she says. "I never meant to hurt you."

"You didn't . . ."

She holds up her hand to stop me. She has to get this out. I think it's been poisoning her for so long, she has to let it go. "I just wanted to be near you."

"But how did you know I'd be here?"

"Mr. Beck knew the whole story. And when he read in the paper that I was getting out, he called the prison and told me he'd heard that Paulina's maid was leaving. He thought you might need me." Her voice cracks and the words come out slow and whispery. "And I didn't want to live if I couldn't be with you."

The wind rattles the window behind my back, and a cold breeze sends a shiver straight through me. I sit here empty-headed, looking into her eyes. "I need to go up to my room for a minute," I say. "I'll be right back."

When I return to the kitchen, Nettie's standing at the sink, scouring a pot with an S.O.S pad that's seen better days. I pick up a dishcloth and start drying a handful of silverware. She looks over at me and sees the gold cross that's sitting just below my blouse collar. Her eyes fill with tears. Then her chin starts to quiver and her voice trembles. "It looks nice on you."

The joy in my heart overwhelms me, and I wrap my arms around her and nuzzle my face into her neck. I have somebody—somebody who's willing to put up with Aunt Paulina treating her like snot to be near me. Nobody could ask for more than that.

And she hugs me back with such force it's as if she never wants to let go. Finally, she holds me at arm's length and smiles huge. "We have a lot of catching up to do."

I nod but don't know where to start.

I guess she doesn't either because now neither of us is saying anything—as if all the words in the entire world have suddenly disappeared. I clear my throat and she plunges her hands back into the dishwater.

"Why don't we listen to the radio," I say, pretending to concentrate on the plate I've rubbed so hard, I'm surprised the roses are still on it.

"Good idea," she says with relief in her voice. She reaches over with a soapy hand and turns the knob to find her favorite station.

The weatherman is telling us there's a nor'easter on the way. "This one'll bring up to eighteen inches," he says with importance in his voice. Give me a break. He's just reading stuff off a paper somebody else wrote. And you know as well as I do that the weather report is your guess is as good as mine.

Next comes a tire commercial and then Patti Page begins to sing "Steam Heat." Nettie starts it, but I can't resist joining in on the *S-sssss* part, so the stiffness that's been hanging in the air disappears. As soon as the song is finished, Nettie looks over at me and says the nicest words in the whole world: "Maybe tomorrow you'll have a snow day."

Fifteen

HOT DAMN! Somebody has decided to give me a present—huge! Aunt Paulina is in the hospital—double pneumonia. The thrill crawls up the back of my neck and leaves a prickly trail of excitement. And an added bonus is that it's winter vacation from school, so I have a full week to bask in the luxury of not having her here. It's as though the doctor asked, *How much time does the kid need? Oh, a week? Well then, that's how long we'll keep the old battle-ax here.* Sometimes you just have to stop and wonder about your good luck.

Nettie has moved into the spare bedroom. Aunt Paulina says I'm too old to need a babysitter but too young to be left alone at night. Besides, I'm sure she made a long list of extra jobs to keep Nettie busy. But I think that having us here, with the run of the house, must be making her itch.

Nettie's as giddy about the situation as I am. She has already made plans for a girls' night out—supper and a movie. Aunt Paulina left a little money to cover our expenses until she gets back. So if Nettie and I stay away from the grocery store and stick with the Dinty Moore beef stew, canned ravioli, and deviled ham that's already in the cupboard, we can live it up in style when we go.

On Friday we'll stop at Howard Johnson for their all-you-can-eat buffet and then go to the Vintage Theater to see *Rear Window*. Nettie loves old movies, and even though he's dead, she's crazy about Jimmy Stewart. Just the mention of his name turns her neck a splotchy pink. The wallet she bought a hundred years ago had a photograph of him in one of those plastic holders, just for show. You are supposed to take the famous person's picture out and replace it with one of your own personal ones. But she left it there like he's her boyfriend.

Nettie and I are on our way to see Aunt Paulina. We get to the hospital at exactly the time visiting hours begin. This is the sort of thing you don't sit at home stewing about. You get it done so you can enjoy the rest of your day.

When we reach Aunt Paulina's floor, the elevator door opens and we're face-to-face with a round-bellied old man with a stubbly face and colorless skin. He's wearing a flimsy hospital gown, no bottoms. "Have you seen my dog?" he asks with a foreign accent. Then, before either of us can say, *No, we haven't,* he pulls his gown over his head and does a little jig dance like a leprechaun. He's wearing expensive loafers and argyle socks—an important person gone loopy.

I have never seen a man's personal property before, and this is definitely not what I expected. Beamer is forever talking about how much fun it must be to *do it.* But I bet she's never seen one of those things either, or she'd stop thinking about it and make cookies or take a walk.

While Nettie's yanking on my arm, a man in a white uniform is running toward us with a blanket in his hands. As I watch the nurse lead the old man away, I hope lightning strikes me before I get like that.

When we go into Aunt Paulina's room, I'm shocked. I thought she would be sitting up, reading *Vanity Fair.* Instead, she's lying flat in bed with her eyes closed—drawn and peaked—almost dead, maybe. This is what I've been wishing for. The sides of the bed are up like a baby's crib, and tubes are stuck up her nose and into her arms with adhesive tape locking them in place.

Nettie must have read my face wrong, because she

puts her hand on my shoulder and says, "She'll be okay. The doctor called this morning. As soon as the medicine has a chance to work, she'll be fine."

But then Mama's nightstand forces its way into my head: the bottles of pills—such pretty colors and so many of them. The memory of how much Mama suffered makes me shudder. The room goes wild like a runaway carnival ride, and I have to get away from this place to keep myself from falling in a heap on the floor.

By the time Nettie catches up with me, I'm standing next to the car, devouring huge breaths of air that don't smell like disinfectant.

When you're a kid whose mother died right in front of you, a storm cloud hovers over your world, waiting to burst wide open and drown you if you let your guard down. Not everybody knows that. The lucky ones don't.

Nettie puts her arms around me. "What's the matter, Katherine?" she says in a quiet voice. "You're shaking."

I'm surprised when I don't burst into tears. My words come out more scared than sad. "When I saw her in the bed like that, all I could think of was my mother and how horrible it was."

Then Nettie starts to cry. "You shouldn't have had to go through that alone. I should have been with you."

Tears stream down my face when I think how much easier it would have been if she'd been there to hold me like this when I felt as if the world were eating me alive.

She takes a Kleenex from her purse, wipes away my tears and then hers. "I'm here now," she says. "And I'm not going anywhere ever again."

Her words wash over me like warm water, and this time I hug her.

BEFORE WE GO to the movies, we stop at Nettie's apartment. It turns out to be one small room, no bathroom even. Everything in it is shabby and drab. There's a couch with blankets and a pillow stacked neatly at one end, a chair, a refrigerator in the corner that's been painted army green to match the walls, and a hot plate on a dresser. Next to the hot plate are six cans of store-brand tomato soup, a nearly empty bag of oyster crackers, a jar of instant coffee, and a box of Cream of Wheat. Everything else must be behind the curtain that's pretending to be a closet door.

While I'm taking inventory of Nettie's belongings, the question I keep asking myself is, *Where does she get the water to make the soup?* The bathroom, I guess, wherever that is. Then I wonder if soup made with bathroom water tastes bad. But that's silly. Sometimes when you're uneasy about a situation, your mind occupies itself with nonsense to calm you down.

"I know it isn't much," Nettie says, apologetic.

I change my face fast, so the look that's making her embarrassed is gone, replaced by a tight smile. "It's pretty," I say.

"Well, I wouldn't call it pretty, but it was the only place I could find ... really all I could afford," she says, fingering the loose cross-stitches on the dresser scarf. "Not everybody wants to rent to someone who's been ... well ... away."

I want so much to tell her that she can come right out and say it, that I think she's a hero for what she did. Instead, I chicken out and head toward the couch, sit down, and make a pretend fuss about how comfortable it is. That's when I see the photographs of me under the glass of the coffee table, a zillion of them from a baby on up, ones I've never seen before.

"Your father brought me a new picture every time he came to visit," she says when she sees me looking at them. "He was so proud of you. He'd spend the whole time telling me about the cute things you'd said and how sweet you were." She sits down next to me and points to the picture where I'm holding up the first-place ribbon from our fourth-grade spelling bee. "This is one of my favorites," she says, resting her chin in her hand and smiling over at me. "He told me how thrilled he was that his daughter was the smartest one in the class and how he took you out for ice cream after the competition. He loved you more than anything in the world. And just look at the beautiful dress he bought for your special night." It's the one Mama made me for Easter, the navy blue and white plaid with the red trim.

I nod, smile, but don't look at her. My eyes would give me away. If I told her he wasn't anywhere near the school that night—that he was passed out drunk in a pool of vomit on the bathroom floor where Mama left him after she couldn't wake him up—it would break her heart.

When lies are all a mother has to make her proud of her son, you do not kill her by telling the truth. "I remember that night," I say, now looking straight into her eyes. "He bought me a double scoop of butterscotch ripple."

WE'RE THE FIRST ONES in the movie theater, and Nettie's trying to decide where she wants to sit. We've already moved twice, and she's turned around in her seat, surveying the auditorium with a pensive look on her face.

"I think the back row would be best after all," she says with conviction in her voice. "I'll get a crick in my neck if I sit this close to the screen. Is that okay with you?"

I've already told her that anywhere is fine with me, but I say, "Sure, I like to sit in the back."

As soon as we're settled, the theater starts filling up. I'm busy devouring my box of Junior Mints when I see Beamer walk down the aisle . . . with a boy—a much older boy wearing tight jeans, one of those short suede jackets with fringe on the sleeves, and a cowboy hat. You can see the faded circle of a chewing tobacco can on his back pocket, and he's walking with a *what the hell* swagger. I guess he thinks he's in Texas. He chooses a seat two rows ahead of us, sits down, parks his boots on the seat in front of him, and starts eating popcorn while Beamer is still standing in the aisle. Before I can catch her eye, the lights go down. She told me she'd met someone at the racetrack when she went to help her father. But she didn't say they were going out. And when I asked her for details, she changed the subject.

"That's a disgrace," Nettie whispers, when the previews begin.

"What is?" I ask, hoping she's talking about the low-cut dress the actress on the screen is wearing.

"That girl ahead of us. She should be ashamed of herself."

"I didn't notice." I'm lying because I haven't taken my eyes off Beamer since she came in. The minute she sat down, whoever that creep is pulled her over and has been mauling her nonstop. The friend in me wants to march right down there and tell him to get off her. But the fact that she's obviously enjoying it and doesn't even care that she's on display in front of people's grandmothers makes me feel as if I am looking at a whole different person.

When the lights come on, Beamer's hair is a royal mess, like when you wake up in the morning after a night of bad dreams. I'm about as disgusted as Nettie, and the fact that she's wearing the new sweater I got with the check Mr. Beck gave me for Christmas makes me feel betrayed. It's the first nice thing I've ever bought with my own money, and I lent it to her, no strings attached, but not to get slobbered all over by him. I will never be able to wear it now with the thought of his hands all over the front. There is a rule when you borrow something. It is to be used just by you.

Nettie has her coat on and has started to leave when suddenly Beamer spins around and looks straight at me. She must have sensed my eyes drilling into her. She searches my face for a second. Then she turns back fast and slides low in her seat. The words I had ready for her lose all their punch when my grown-up side informs my high-and-mighty side that she does not have to ask my permission to have a personal life.

Sixteen

It's two in the morning and I can't sleep. Miss Plain asked me to come to school early today. She wants to talk to me about something. I think it must have to do with the national writing competition I overheard her discussing with the principal. The winner will get a thousand dollars and a trip to Washington, D.C., to meet the president. Just imagine having your picture in all the papers, shaking hands with the president of the United States!

I'm lying on my bed, chewing a whole box of Chiclets and reading *A Tree Grows in Brooklyn*. I didn't think I'd ever find a book as good as *To Kill a Mockingbird*, but here it is right in front of me. Don't ask me which one I like better, because as far as I'm concerned, they're both perfect.

I'm at the part where Francie's father dies, and I'm about one second away from dying myself. I'm sobbing so hard that my bed is shaking, and my heart feels as if it's about to crumble into dust. For heaven's sake, her life's been hard enough without that happening. But I guess an author can do what she wants with her own book. I just would have written it differently. Maybe the daddy could have gotten really sick and almost died. But in the end, he would have pulled through, and the mother would have appreciated what a nice husband she had and treated him better. Of course, he would have stopped drinking and gotten a steady job so Mrs. Nolan wouldn't have had to scrub floors and worry about where their next meal was coming from. But then I wouldn't be here blubbering because I love this book so much. So I guess Betty Smith knew what she was doing after all.

It amazes me how a writer can work magic with words, making the characters so real that you forget they were just made up in somebody's head. And the best ones make you feel as though you're part of the story, living in the family's spare room. Of course, the Nolans didn't have a spare room, but you know what I mean.

I think how Francie's father was a drunk like mine, only hers had a soft side and he knew how to show love. I guess that's what makes all the difference.

As I'm wiping my eyes on the edge of the pillowcase, whispers in my head remind me how strange it is that I can cry buckets for a pretend girl's father, but I couldn't squeeze out one measly tear for my own. Maybe the tears I'm crying for Francie aren't for her at all. But I won't let myself go there—not right now. What good would it do?

Sometimes I think I might have been put together wrong. Like the way I feel better on dark days and when it rains, and how my taste in books is weird for a girl my age. I don't have any use for light and funny. I don't even read the comics in the newspaper like regular people. There's nothing in those little boxes that comes anywhere near real life. I'd rather be strangled than read the smoochy stories the swoony-eyed girls in school drool over. I like sad and dark—troubled characters with empty cupboards and empty souls.

The only thing Beamer reads are love comics, and she gets all empty eyed and antsy if I even mention a book I'm reading. So I keep that part of my life to myself, except with Miss Plain. When she doesn't have a meeting or something else to do, I get to school early, help her pass out homework papers, and we talk about what we're reading. Hers right now is a book of Dorothy Parker's poetry. And, well ... I just told you what mine is. Those times make me feel as if my heart is being fed a full-course meal. If you gave me a choice of being with Miss Plain discussing books and just about anything else—you know which one I'd choose.

———

TODAY WHEN I enter the classroom, Miss Plain is standing at the board, writing a list of vocabulary words. Usually she finishes what she's working on, but today is different. She puts the chalk back on the tray and tells me to hang up my coat and sit at my desk. Whatever this is about, it's serious. I can tell by her face.

"I've been thinking about this for some time, Katherine," she says in a funeral voice. She's sitting sideways on the seat of the desk in front of mine. She's wearing her dark green suit, the one with the black velvet collar and cuffs. It's too dressy for school, but maybe she doesn't have any place else to wear it. She has on her gold circle pin, but no other jewelry. We're in the row next to the window, and the sun is making her hair shimmer. I don't know what to expect, so I don't know how to feel. I wait and say nothing.

"I'm worried about you, Katherine," she says, as she rises from her chair a little, adjusts her skirt, then sits back down. My hands are folded on my desk. She pats them lightly.

This is the first time a teacher has ever made the effort to have a heart-to-heart with me, and I think how considerate that is. But I know where this is probably leading, and I don't want to follow.

After my father was killed and my mother got so sick, my old school brought in an expert to work on my head so I wouldn't fall apart and scare the other kids. When you are ready to burst wide open at the seams, meeting with a strange man in a black suit every week just gives you one more thing to worry about. Besides, I am not what you would call the open type, so the school might as well have saved its money and the shrink's time.

It doesn't take long to figure out how to make yourself sound okay. When he gives you a word and you have to say the first thing that comes into your head, you take the upbeat path. Like if he says *mother,* of course the first thing you would think of would be *dead.* But you say *father* to throw him off. And when he shows you the inkblot that looks like a monster holding a knife in his raised hand, you see a lady sitting in a chair with a feather in her hat. Pretty soon he will lose interest, and you will be able to go back to art class on Friday afternoons. And nobody will notice that the paperweight you are making out of clay looks a lot like a heart with a crack in it.

I'm ready to tell Miss Plain how great I feel when she tosses me a ball I can't catch. "I don't think you should associate with Bernadette Talson," she says straight-out, not even a question in her voice. "She's headed for trouble, and I'm afraid she's planning on taking you with her." Her eyes mean business and make mine look down.

The fact that Beamer loves Miss Plain as much as I do makes me feel like crying. She takes people as they come and doesn't expect them to fit in the right slot.

What Miss Plain doesn't know is that I need Beamer a whole lot more than she needs me. Besides, your mind can't tell your heart how to feel. Maybe she hasn't learned that rule yet.

"So let's move your things down front," Miss Plain says. She gets up from her chair and smoothes out her skirt. "I spoke with some of the girls yesterday, and they agreed to take you under their wings. You're at the age where who you choose to be your friends can determine your future." She checks my face to make sure I'm taking in every word. "And you have a lot going for you, Katherine. It would be a shame to throw it all away."

She's halfway down the aisle with my books when words I didn't know were coming shoot out of my mouth. "I've already chosen my friend, Miss Plain. I want to stay here." Then I add, "If that's all right with you," for politeness.

She looks at me as if I smacked her in the head. She was only doing what was best for me is what I know she's thinking. But now she has this ingrate on her hands, and it's too much of an effort to try anymore. "If you're sure that's what you want," she says, walking back toward my desk, placing my books down gently.

I know I'm now at the end of the line for a place in her heart. But I *am* flattered that she wanted me to be in her club. The dues were just too high.

Seventeen

I DON'T KNOW if you knew this or not, but grown-ups can actually get the measles. Nettie's living proof of that fact. She's quarantined in her apartment for a week. And Aunt Paulina's home from the hospital on bed rest, so it doesn't take Sherlock Holmes to figure out where that leaves me.

Aunt Paulina called the school when she first got home to tell them I'm down with the flu and not to expect me for quite a while. My heart sank into my shoes when I heard her say that. The two of us alone together is not something I would sit up nights wishing for. But the fact that she can tell a great big, bald-faced lie makes me envy her a little. I guess she didn't have a Sunday school teacher who drummed it into her head that God punishes people for doing things like that. When you're afraid that a magical person who can make you burn in hell is watching your every move, it takes some of the fun out of life.

They say when a sick person starts to get grumpy, it means she's getting better. With Aunt Paulina, it's hard to tell. But I think she's on the road to recovery. "Bring me this, bring me that," she says a million times a day. Right now I'm on my way into her room with three pills and a glass of ginger ale.

It would have been so much easier if she had stayed in the hospital like the doctor wanted her to. But, oh no. She knows better than anybody what's good for her, and everybody else can go to hell.

"I've been ringing the bell," she says, as I'm rearranging the whatnots and laying the medicine out on the nightstand. "Why didn't you come?"

"I was doing up your breakfast dishes and having a bite for myself. It's only eight o'clock. I'm going as fast as I can." If I were punching a time clock, I would already have two hours toward a paycheck. And as far as the bell she uses to get me to run in her direction, it is only the second morning and I am ready to smack her with it. As soon as she falls asleep, it's going to disappear.

"I need my bed changed," she says, running her hands through hair that has given up trying. Her face has taken on a gaunt, weaselly shape, and the sickness has run off with the color and left a huge crusty sore by the side of her mouth. "You were supposed to do that after my breakfast. There's coffee all over the sheet."

I stare down at her face until she lowers her eyes. It's my turn to talk, but I don't say anything. I make her wait and enjoy the fact that now she's the one who's sunk to the bottom instead of Mama. Then I think how thoughtful it would be if she would just die.

"And my hair's filthy. Will you wash it for me?"

Just the thought of touching her head gives me the creeps. "The doctor said you'll be strong enough to take a shower in a few days. You can wash your own hair, then."

She doesn't throw the fit I expected. Instead, she just lies there. Then her chin starts to quiver and tears spill onto the pillow. She looks up at me with such pitiful eyes that she reminds me of a cur dog in my old town. The one everybody was afraid of. But then one day he was hit by a truck and left in the street to die. You could see relief on their faces as people passed by, stopping only long enough to make sure that he was busted up beyond repair. His eyes are what I remember most, and of course, the fact that something terrible must have happened to make him so mean. Puppies don't come into the world snapping and growling. But I know what made Aunt Paulina mean.

I also know what Mama would have done if she were here.

"I'll wash your hair in the bathroom sink," I say. I take one of her fancy lace handkerchiefs from a bureau drawer and dab her eyes with it. "I'll be right back." Before I turn toward the door, I tuck the hanky into her rolled-up fist. I'm pretty sure the fortress she built to hold her feelings back from the world is about to crumble. And that's not a time when you want an audience gawking at you, so I leave fast and head downstairs for a water pitcher and a folding chair.

AUNT PAULINA is calm now, satisfied, I think, to have nice-smelling hair again and a person waiting on her hand and foot. "You're a good girl, Katherine," she says. There's nothing in her eyes to suggest that she's speaking from anywhere but her heart, and the kind words don't stick in her throat. "Thank you for taking such good care of me."

She slipped this one past me. I wasn't ready for it. "Oh, right," I say, just before I realize that doesn't make sense. But something inside of me relaxes, tells me just to go with it. Maybe it's how soldiers feel when the war is over, even when they lose.

AUNT PAULINA'S up and around, and she's treating Nettie and me like real people, which feels strange but kind of nice. I have a feeling her brush with death softened her heart and cleaned the spite out of her soul, at least for a little while. I'd love to ask her why she was so angry with Nettie, but I guess that's none of my business. Besides, if I wait long enough, I'll find out. I bet someday Nettie will stop ignoring my hints and tell me herself.

"Kat?" I hear from the kitchen. Nettie's snipping artichokes for supper, and I'm in the dining room, setting the table for three. The one minus thing about the new-and-improved Aunt Paulina is this eating arrangement. She calls it dining together—what well-bred families do. And she can't very well chew on a sirloin steak while Nettie and I are eating tuna-noodle casserole, even though that's exactly what we'd both rather be doing. So there go the cozy suppers at the kitchen table with just Nettie and me, talking about ordinary things and making cracks about the old Aunt Paulina.

"Did you want something?" I call back to Nettie. I expect her to remind me that the forks go on the left, which I have known since I was a baby. My mother taught me how to set a table. When you are like Mama, raised in a house with manners, you carry them with you through your life, even if you spend it in a hundred-dollar-a-month flat above a shoe repair.

"I forgot to tell you," Nettie says. "Someone named Bernadette phoned while you were at the Becks'. She wants you to call her. She said it's important."

I walk over to the kitchen door and give myself a minute. "Okay, thanks," I say in a casual voice like people leave messages for me all the time. "It's just a girl from school," I say. "She probably wants the homework assignments. She was absent today." But I know that isn't it. Beamer never calls here. Besides, she's been acting strange lately, asking me a bunch of questions I don't know the answers to.

My mood sinks and I'm losing my appetite for the twice-baked potatoes Nettie has in the oven. It's weird how sometimes your mind knows a thing ahead of time— and it lets you in on it slowly, so you don't die of shock.

Eighteen

IT's HARD TO believe that Beamer is in such deep trouble, because if you don't count the way her face has turned old, her body looks the same, no hint that there's a real live person inside her. It's Saturday and we're on a bus headed to the Women's Center in Montpelier to find out what she should do. Beamer used the money her father gave her for new sneakers to buy the tickets, and I told Aunt Paulina I was going to spend the day at the library, which was a tiny bit true. On the way to the bus station, we passed it and I ran in and returned a book.

Beamer is sitting there looking out the window at nothing. There's no pretty scenery anyway, just a lumber mill and miles of junk cars piled on top of each other like squashed soda cans. I think she has turned her mind off like you do a radio when you have listened to the newscaster drone on about a depressing subject and you can't stand to hear his voice one second longer.

This is a time when you leave the down person alone. Like when somebody has died, you do not try to cheer up the mourners by cracking jokes. You just stay quiet and available, in case they decide they want to talk. It is their call.

I look over at Beamer and feel that there is depth to a friendship when you can sit with a person and say nothing—not have to fill the edgy air with useless talk. Then I settle back in my seat, lay my head against the paper head protector, and think about our conversation the day before.

"But how do you know?" I asked. We were sitting on the front steps of the funeral home because Weesie shares Beamer's room and she kept coming in, wanting to know what we were talking about.

She stared down at her clenched hands and shrugged. "I just know."

"But how?"

She looked over at me and got all mad sounding. "Well, for starters, I'm two months late."

"That doesn't mean anything." I don't know what I'm talking about, but I have to say something.

"I'm *always* twenty-eight days. You could set your clock."

"Well, maybe this is just a fluke."

"Yeah, some *fluke*. Plus, I feel crappy. My stomach's all bloated and I'm queasy and I've never had so many zits in my life."

"People get zits when they're pregnant?"

"I don't know. I guess. I didn't look like this before."

I tried to cheer her up by making my voice sound happy. "You might have the flu."

It didn't work. "That's what my mother thought. And seven months later Weesie was born."

Then I changed to the other side of the problem. "Does Randy know?" That's his name. Randy Wade. Randy the good-for-nothing jerk is more like it.

She sighs. "Yeah, he knows."

"And?"

"He said to get lost. Not to bother him again."

"What?!"

"He told me it was *my* problem. To take care of it."

I look over at Beamer and think how she actually loved that guy. And how she thought he loved her back. "He told me I was pretty," she said one day in the cafeteria. "Nobody's ever done that before."

According to Mama, this is the girl's number-one nightmare—even worse than most diseases. I don't think she thought about how it would make me feel—that she would rather have had tuberculosis or something than be unmarried and pregnant with me. But there's an ache in my throat when I think how it turned out. She loved me as big as the sky is how she used to put it.

WE'RE SITTING in the waiting room of the Women's Center. I'm looking around at the other people, trying to guess what they're here for, and Beamer's flipping through a pamphlet about breast-feeding. She lets out a huge sigh, then puts the brochure in her pocket and starts jiggling her leg fast. "My God, Kat, if they don't call me pretty soon, I'm going to . . ."

"Bernadette Talson?" A woman wearing a white uniform is standing next to us, speaking softly.

Beamer jumps up. "Yes. That's me."

The woman puts her hand on Beamer's arm and leads her toward the back of the clinic.

As I watch her walk away, I think that God shouldn't make it possible for young girls to get pregnant. So this is really his fault. He's so squeaky-clean perfect. He has no idea how regular people feel when he pulls dirty tricks like this on them.

When Beamer comes back, I search her face. She looks blank, like she's not thinking anything. She sits next to me, staring at a poster on the wall of a scared-looking young girl, cradling her enormous belly. And that's when the flood comes. She buries her head in her lap and starts that quiet sobbing where your whole body shakes but no sound comes out. I lean down, rub her back, and tell her how sorry I am. When she's finished, she says, "I need to go home right now. There's an early bus."

As we're leaving, she takes the breast-feeding flyer out of her pocket and puts it back on the table. Maybe she's not going to have the baby. But that would be a huge Catholic sin. That can't be it. Then I tell myself to cut it out. Sometimes I'm just so tiresome. I'll have the whole story written before it even happens.

We're halfway to the bus station, and I can't stand the quiet another minute. "So? What happened?" I'm out of breath from trying to keep up with her.

She keeps walking. "I'm not pregnant."

I grab her arm and make her stop. "What?"

"I'm not pregnant. The doctor said it happens sometimes. It could have been from worrying about it or maybe just because I'm young. She gave me something to start my cycle again."

"But aren't you happy about it?" I say, wondering what's going on here. "You seem sadder than you were before."

"I don't know how I feel. I was just so scared. I don't think it's sunk in yet."

Well, I sure know how *I* feel—all light and happy inside and nobody to share it with.

We start walking, regular speed this time. She lets out a short little "Huh," then says, "My family's just hanging together by a thread as it is. This would have done it for sure."

Good. She's talking. I have to let her lead or she might clam up again.

"Every time I do something wrong, my mother just loves to remind me about the thirty-five hours of agonizing labor she went through to have me."

I see a stone on the sidewalk, kick it a little ways, then again, harder.

"I guess when you're grown-up and ready for it, it's a good thing," she says. "I just can't believe how close I came to making a complete mess of everything."

She looks better now and she's breathing right. I'll take a chance. "I'm glad everything turned out okay."

"Oh," she moans. "So am I." She stops and looks up at the sky. "Thank you, God. I don't know what I did to deserve this, but thank you." Then she turns to me and hugs me so tight, I can't breathe. "And thanks for coming, Kat. I couldn't have done this alone."

"That's okay."

"And, Kat?"

"What?"

"Thanks for not judging me."

———

BEAMER SLEEPS all the way home. When we get off the bus, I say, "Do you want to go get a soda or something?" This calls for a celebration is what I'm thinking.

"Maybe some other time." She has a faraway look. "Right now I have to go hug my father."

What she said surprises me. "Does he know about this?"

"No. I didn't even tell him I was seeing Randy."

"But what about when you went out on dates?"

"I told him I was meeting you."

She is the most complicated girl I have ever met. "So then why do you have to hug him?"

She looks deep into my eyes and smiles. "He would have been there for me."

Nineteen

THE MOST AMAZING thing has happened. Aunt Paulina
has a boyfriend. His name is Maxwell Stone. He's about
her age, tall, and has the same color hair and eyes as my
father. Plus, he likes kids, especially girls. He has a daughter about my age that he never sees because his ex-wife
turned her against him. The day he moved to Ellenville,
he came to the house and asked Aunt Paulina if he could
use the phone to call a service station because his car had
broken down. I thought she'd shoo him away and slam the
door. But no, she let him come in, gave him coffee and
cookies, and invited him back for dinner.

Today Max is taking Aunt Paulina across Lake
Champlain on a ferry. Then they're going to Saratoga so

he can show her how to double her money on the horses. I haven't figured out what I'm going to do yet, but Nettie's staying here with the long face she's been wearing since Max came into our lives. She won't say what she doesn't like about him, just that she can tell a rat when she sees one. I've tried to convince her that she's wrong, but I have a feeling that after what she's been through, all men look like rats to her.

I'M IN MY ROOM about to go through Mama's keepsakes. They've been in my closet, locked in her suitcase. Until today I couldn't look at them because the wound was still too fresh. But the time comes when you can do a thing. You just have to wait until your heart tells you it's ready.

When I open the lid of the box I'm holding, the scent of cedar comes out strong. It is one of those wooden chests they sell in souvenir shops along with fake peace pipes, rubber hunting knives, and burlap sachets that smell like balsam with the name of the town you are visiting printed across the front in green paint.

I pour the things onto my bed and scatter them around in a circle. I pick up the hospital wristband from when I had my tonsils out and put it next to the little plastic bag of my baby teeth. Then I examine the Canadian two-dollar coin my father got in change when he took us to an amusement park near Montreal. That was such a fun time. He was sober and in a good mood. Everything was perfect, even the ride home.

"Kat?" It's Nettie calling through the door, knocking a little at the same time. She is polite that way and never barges in like Aunt Paulina. I bet she's going to tell me lunch is ready. She is trying out a new recipe she found in *Homemaker's Digest*—hot chicken salad. When she told me about it, I thought, *Yuck. Why don't we just do cold? We* know *that's good.* But then I saw the magazine on the kitchen counter. I read the ingredients and I like every single one of them. And as an added bonus, you get scrunched-up potato chips sprinkled on top. A photograph of the finished product showed it all brown and crispy, nestled in a bright orange bowl. Next to it was a dark blue napkin folded into a triangle with a pewter fork sitting on top as if to say, *Go ahead, try it. It's as good as it looks.* Nettie won't fuss with the presentation part. That's what they call it when you put extra effort into making it look appetizing—presentation. She'll just serve it on a regular plate and leave the Pyrex casserole dish on the stove. And I don't think she'll bother with the tossed salad and the crusty roll. Maybe some tomato slices or pickled beets from a jar.

"Come in," I say. Before, I would have made her wait until I had everything put back and out of sight. But now that she's part of me, we can share.

She opens the door slowly but stays where she is. "I just wanted to let you know that lunch will be ready in about half an hour." She's smiling, but there's something else. I'm not sure what it is. She shifts feet and checks the waistband of her apron. Maybe she's lonely—the waiting time between putting the food in the oven and sitting down to eat.

"It smells good," I say. I can't smell anything. I just think she needs a lift.

"But I just . . . Oh, thank you." She knows I'm fibbing but appreciates the thought. "Well, I hope it's okay. I'm usually not one for trying new things. It just looked so good in the picture."

"Do you want to come in?" I ask. "I'm sorting through some of my mother's things."

She backs up fast. "Oh, sweetie," she says with her hand over her heart, "I didn't know. I'll leave you alone."

"No, that's all right." I say. "You don't have to go."

She anchors her hair behind her ears and straightens her back. "Are you sure?"

"I'm sure." I pat a spot on the bed next to me.

She touches my hair lightly before she sits down. "What is it you're looking at?"

I hand her a photograph of my mother, standing next to our Christmas tree. She's wearing a scarf I knitted for her when I was about six, an ugly yellow and burnt orange thing.

Nettie holds the photo at arm's length, studies it for a long time, then looks at me. "Your father used to tell me what a good mother she was and how nice she kept your house. I'm sorry I never got to meet her."

I nod. I'm sorry, too. She would have loved her as much as I did.

"And I recognize that scarf. Jacob wore his all one winter when he came to see me. I couldn't believe you made it. You were just a tiny little thing then."

I'd forgotten that I knitted them each one. Mama said it was too pretty to wear and kept it in her drawer for something good to come up. But *good* never came. And I didn't know that Daddy wore his right out in public.

I smile and hand her a picture of me standing next to my first bike.

She glances at the photo, then puts it on her lap. Her face goes serious and there's fear in her voice when she says, "Did your father ever . . . ?" She stops to take a deep breath, then tries again. "What I mean is, was you father ever mean?"

I see Mama on the floor, begging for him to stop. I hear him laughing at the top of the roller coaster, putting his arm around me so I wouldn't be scared. And there's Nettie with hope in her eyes, waiting for an answer. A voice in my head says, *Don't! What would be the point?* "No, he wasn't mean."

There's a freckle on my arm I didn't see before. It looks a little like a tiny oak leaf.

She lets out a heavy breath and her shoulders relax. "I was just wondering because of all the ugliness he went through. And then he had to go to that awful place. You hear those stories about kids growing up and doing the same terrible things that were done to them." Her eyes get all watery. She takes off her glasses and wipes the tears with the hem of her apron. "He was such a sweet little boy. I'm glad that didn't happen to him."

I reach over and put my hand on hers. "I remember the day he taught me how to ride that bike. We had a good time."

She sighs. "Thank god," she says, closing her eyes. "I don't think I could stand it if I thought you or your mother had to go through any of that."

I can't let her go any deeper. I might end up telling her the truth, and she doesn't need any more grief than what she's already gone through. I gather Mama's treasures together and put them back into the box. Then I take in a breath, let it out fast, and lighten my voice. "Do you think lunch is almost ready? I'm starving."

WELL, THIS IS DISGUSTING. Even the potato chips can't save it. I don't think mayonnaise is supposed to be heated up. The magazine people must not have tried this one out before they printed it.

"What do you think?" Nettie's sitting across from me. I can't read her face.

I push a little pile of the stuff around on my plate. "It's really pretty . . ."

"Awful," Nettie says, without missing a beat. "It's just terrible. I don't know what I did wrong."

I lay my fork down, relieved. "I don't think you did anything wrong. It's just a bad recipe."

Nettie stands up, gathers our plates, and heads for the sink. "It's too bad we don't have a dog. I hate to throw out good food."

Even a dog would walk away from this. Besides, this is definitely not good food. "It's not your fault," I say. "The magazine shouldn't fool people like that."

"Kat?" Nettie's holding back the curtain, looking out the window.

"What?"

"The Beck boy is in the backyard." Her voice is at low volume, confidential. "He's wearing a strange outfit. And, well, he's just . . . I don't know, staring at the house."

I walk over to the window. Johnny's sitting cross-legged under the elm tree. He has his magician's hat on and the black cape that came with the set. His elbows are on his knees, and he's tapping on his cheek with the plastic wand.

I head for the door. "He's not supposed to be out by himself. As soon as he sees me, he'll go home." I call to him. He stays where he is. "That's not like him," I tell Nettie. "I'll be right back."

As soon as I reach the tree, Johnny says, "Do you want to see a trick?" He spoke right out as if this is nothing new. Mr. Beck was right. It takes awhile, but he does come around.

"Sure," I answer. "I love tricks." I point to the grass next to him. "Is it okay if I sit down?"

"Yeah." He nods fast. "Yeah."

I get settled. "I'm ready," I say. "Work your magic."

"Okay. Okay." He has a rope in his lap. There's a knot at one end. "You have to close your eyes so I can get ready. And no peeking." I haven't heard this excitement in his voice before.

I squeeze my eyes shut and cover them with my hands. "I can't see a thing."

"Okay. Now!" He's holding the rope up. The knot's at the bottom. He looks at it and frowns. "Wait. Wait. You have to close your eyes again."

I do.

"Now I'm ready. You can look." He's holding the rope at each end. The knot's hidden in his fist, showing a little. He shakes the rope close to my face. "See? Just a plain rope. No knot."

I nod. "You're right. I don't see a knot anywhere."

He laughs, then drops the knotted end of the rope. "Tah-dah! Magic!"

I clap and make a surprised face. "Wow! How'd you do that?"

"Papa showed me. I have one with a penny, but I'm not good enough yet."

He looks over my shoulder and his face changes. Nettie's walking toward us with a tray of sandwiches and milk. "I brought you a snack," she says. She glances up at the plain blue sky. "It's such a nice warm day. I thought a picnic was in order." She puts the tray on the grass between Johnny and me, then turns toward Johnny. "I hope you like grilled cheese."

She looks at me, wondering. I nod yes. Johnny's face lights up.

"Nettie, this is Johnny Beck," I say. "Johnny, this is Nettie."

"It's nice to meet you, Johnny," Nettie says.

"Yeah," he says, but doesn't look at her. He's busy watching the food. Then he jumps up, grabs a glass of milk, and hightails it toward his house, leaving a white trail behind him.

"I'm sorry," Nettie says. "I guess I scared him off."

For a minute I think she's right, but then I think no. He was different this time. "It's nothing you did," I say. "It's just his way. Besides, I have a feeling he'll be back."

"Well then. I'll get out of here. I don't want to make it any harder on him than it already is." As I watch her go toward the house, I realize that some people just know.

I'm thinking how hot it is and that summer vacation's almost here when I hear Johnny running across the lawn. This time he's leaving a trail of chocolate milk. He sits down and smiles. "Want me to do yours, too?" he asks.

I smile back. "No, that's okay. Maybe next time."

"Yeah. Maybe next time," he says, reaching for a sandwich.

Twenty

I FINISHED my homework and now I'm sitting on the front-porch swing, doing a crossword puzzle. I'm trying to think of a four-letter word for *feet* when Max comes out with a pitcher of lemonade and three glasses. "Hope you don't mind company," he says. "It's too nice a night to waste it inside." He still has his own apartment, but I don't know why. He spends most of his time here.

"Sure, come on out." I was enjoying my alone time, and that third glass tells me the whole thing will be pure wrecked as soon as Aunt Paulina gets here. I bet she's drowning her hair with gel. There's a tiny breeze that might move something. And you can be sure that coming outside was not her idea.

He sits down next to me and puts the lemonade on the table in front of us. I still have my feet on it, but, boy, I'll get them off fast when I hear her coming. "So," he says, "doing a crossword puzzle, huh?"

Well, I *was*. Not anymore. I am one of those people who can't stand to have anybody try to help. I close the book. "Just finished," I say, tapping the cover with the pencil. This is the first time we've been alone together. When you're just beginning, it's hard to know what to say. I look over and give him one of those *oh, well* smiles where your closed mouth stretches out long and your eyebrows rise like mountaintops.

"I guess school is almost out," he says. He's wearing a gold ring with a dark blue stone on his pinky finger. I've never seen it before. Then I remember the Tiffany package that came in the mail.

"Yup," I say. "Just a few more weeks."

He picks up the pitcher and starts pouring. "I suppose you'll be spending most of the summer at the beach."

"The beach? I didn't know they had one here."

"Oh, sure. It's beautiful. Right down at the end of Wallworth Street. A five-minute walk." He hands me a glass of lemonade. "Isn't that what girls your age do? Spend the summer working on your tans, wearing those little . . ."

I think it might be time to leave.

"You were right. It *is* nice out, Max." Aunt Paulina's standing next to me, glaring at my shoes. How'd she get out here without making any noise? She's wearing her dress-up heels, so she must have put some effort into it.

I tuck my feet under the swing and wait for the right time to excuse myself. I'll have a lot of homework to do, maybe have to study for a huge test. I look up at her. "Do you want to sit here?" I start to stand. I'll tell my fib and keep on going.

Max reaches for my arm and holds it down. "You're all settled, Katherine," he says. "Paulie can sit *here*." He pulls a white wicker rocker over next to him and pats the thick periwinkle cushion. Inside her head I bet she is stewing good.

She hesitates but then sees his arm draped across the back of the chair and walks toward him with a smile on her face. He waits for her to sit down, then hands her a lemonade and rubs the back of her neck. She takes a drink. "This is delicious, Max. I didn't know you could cook."

He laughs and then pulls her over and massages her neck with both hands. He looks at me. "Your aunt's got a real good sense of humor."

"Right," I say. I look at Aunt Paulina. "That *was* funny." I have to get out of here.

She moves in her chair a little and lowers her head. "Well, I . . ."

"Ah, come on, Paulie. Don't be modest. It's one of the things I find so attractive about you." He grabs the back of her head and gives her a smash kiss that makes her nose go flat.

Oh, puke. It's definitely time for me to leave. I scoot to the edge of my seat and take my puzzle book from the table. "Well," I say, "I really have to go."

"But it's early," Max says. "It's not even dark yet. Besides, I was just going to tell your aunt that you were a big part of the reason I fell in love with her."

Well, now, this is getting interesting. I lean back. "I was?"

"Absolutely."

Aunt Paulina's eyes dart at me, then over to Max. Her face has kind of all fallen apart. She pulls her hand away from his and says, "What are you talking about?"

He swallows the last of his drink and then stares down at the empty glass. "This isn't easy for a man to say, but I was lonely. I wanted a family."

Aunt Paulina's face has softened some. Max reaches over, takes her hand back, and looks square at her. "I knew the minute I saw you that you were the one. But I wanted a child." He shakes his head. "And you know that's impossible for me."

Well, I didn't need to hear that. But, wait. He has a daughter. Oh. She's probably adopted.

Max clears his throat and keeps staring into Aunt Paulina's eyes. "So, when I found out you had Katherine, I figured it was meant to be. And now I know that it was."

Well, imagine that. All of a sudden I have become valuable.

"Let's go inside, Max," Aunt Paulina says. "I'm getting a little cold."

"Sure, hon, I was just thinking the same thing." Max gets up, holds out his hands, and pulls Aunt Paulina up from her chair. As they're leaving, she looks my way, not mean, but I can tell the wheels in her head are turning hard.

IT'S STARTING to get dark, and there's a dog down the street that's barking like crazy. I guess I'll go inside and get ready for bed. Then I'll read for a while. Wait! That's it. I open my crossword book. Yup, I was right. It fits. I write down *dogs* for six across.

Just as I'm opening the door to go in, I hear Beamer say my name.

I jump, then whisper, "What are you doing here? You scared me."

"Sorry, but you told me you spend a lot of time on the porch. I tried calling, but nobody answered. I figured maybe you were out here."

I close the door and tell Beamer to sit on the swing.

"I'm glad you came. You just startled me is all. What's the matter?"

Her face is solid serious. "My mother left. She's going to divorce my father."

Out of the blue like this. What's a person supposed to say? "She is?"

"He's not exciting enough. And she hates Ellenville. She says it's smothering her. She's wanted to leave for a long time."

"Really? That's awful!"

"She didn't even tell him in person. When I got home from school, I found a note on the table. *I* had to be the one to break the news."

"But where did she go?"

"California."

Oh my gosh! I thought maybe Bennington. I have to say something encouraging. "Maybe she'll come back."

Her voice breaks. "But she took Weesie with her. To Hollywood. On a bus for god's sake. So she can be discovered."

Okay, so that's what the tears are for. "That's terrible. Do you think Weesie even wanted to go?" I ask.

She looks at me as if I should know better. "That wouldn't make any difference. My mother's the boss."

Then I think how much money that would take. "But where are they going to stay?"

"With my aunt Kate in Pasadena until they can afford a place of their own. Kate's my mother's older sister. She's a librarian, if you can believe that." She wipes her eyes with the cuff of her blouse, then takes a deep breath. "At least Weesie'll be okay till my father can get her back. She didn't even take her Barbies, so I bet my mother told her they were just going for a visit."

I'm wondering how Mr. Talson's going to get Weesie back when Beamer says, "I've got to go. My father's a mess." She laughs a little through her nose. "I don't know. I just had to tell you."

And before I can say anything, she bounds off the step and starts running full speed down the street.

I feel a tiny bit guilty saying this, but I think California is the perfect place for Mrs. Talson. I guess it's where she's always wanted to be. But tears start as I picture Weesie when her mother tells her she won't be coming back.

Twenty-One

MR. BECK'S in the living room, reading the chapter we just finished, and I'm in the kitchen playing checkers with Johnny so he'll leave his grandfather alone.

"King me!" he says with a big grin on his face.

"Not yet. You have to . . ."

"King me!" He's flapping his hands and jiggling up and down on his chair.

"We haven't even started. You have to move one of your men so we can play."

"Which one?"

"Any one."

"Okay, here goes. Now king me."

"No, that's mine. You have to move a black one."

"Move it where?"

"Just one space."

He looks at me and frowns.

"Like this." I move one of his checkers.

"Okay. Okay." He moves it another square.

"No, not yet. It's my turn." I move his checker back. "You have to wait until *I* move a man."

"Why?"

"Because that's the way you play. Just watch." I move one of mine. "Now it's your turn."

He moves his checker next to mine and smiles.

I start to explain, but change my mind, jump his man, and take his checker. "See? That's how you win. You try to get all the other person's men."

He folds his arms, squints his eyes, and speaks in a tight voice. "I want my checker back."

"No, that's not the way it works. You have to try to get some of mine."

"That's *my* checker. You said the black ones were mine."

"Yes, but . . ." I sigh and hand him the checker. "Okay, now it's your turn."

Johnny's grin is back and Mr. Beck is standing in the doorway. He laughs. "Not easy, is it?"

I smile and shake my head.

Johnny runs over to Mr. Beck. "Papa, where's that toy paper?"

"I thought you were playing checkers," Mr. Beck says, winking at me. "You usually play longer than that."

"We're done." He holds up the checker. "I won. Now I want to see the toys."

MR. BECK and I are at the typewriter and Johnny's looking at a toy flyer from the newspaper. "Here's the train I want, Papa. This big one right here." He slams the paper on the dining-room table and pats it.

Mr. Beck slides the flyer over and scrutinizes the picture. "Ah, so that's the one you've been telling me about. That *is* a beauty."

"Yeah. Do you think that beauty could come here for my birthday?"

"Well, you never know. I guess you'll have to wait and find out." Mr. Beck props his elbow on the table, rests his chin on the heel of his hand, and looks over at Johnny with love on his face. "You know what I've been thinking?"

"What?"

"Maybe we could take a ride on a real train when summer comes."

Johnny's face wakes up. "Like how we did with Nana? To the big city with all the lights?"

"That's the place."

He takes the flyer back and stares at the picture. "But do you think this train right here will come to this house for my birthday?"

JOHNNY'S IN HIS ROOM, and Mr. Beck and I are a good way into another chapter when he stops dictating and says, "You remind me so much of your mother."

He might as well have taken his heart out and handed it to me. "I do?"

"You have her long fingers, and your chin is shaped the same. And you crawl into people's hearts just the way she did."

I smile and hope he says more.

"She was just the sweetest little thing, always wanted to please everybody. She and Lily did everything together." He chuckles. "I remember one April Fool's Day. They were in about sixth grade. They put salt in the sugar bowl and then made me a cup of coffee. They sat there and watched me put in two heaping spoonfuls of the stuff and then take a big drink. They thought it was the funniest thing in the world."

"What did you do?"

"Well, after I rinsed my mouth, I congratulated them. It was the first year they really got me. The other times I just pretended to be fooled."

I think how my father would have reacted and how I wouldn't have dared to do such a thing in the first place.

I wait for a minute before I ask the question that's been festering in me for as long as I can remember. "Why did my grandparents just throw her away?"

He sees the tears in my eyes, reaches over, and puts his hand on mine. "Your grandfather had rules he expected people to live by. And when your mother didn't follow those rules . . . well, he was a stubborn man."

"But what about my grandmother? Why didn't she do something?"

It's as if he's not going to answer, but then changes his mind. "Those rules applied to her, too."

He leans toward me and opens his arms. While he's hugging me, I wish all the men in the world were just like Mr. Beck.

Twenty-Two

"SHE MIGHT AS WELL scrape gum off the sidewalk and bring it on home." Nettie's sitting at the kitchen table, shucking peas, and her eyes are spitting fire. A pea ricochets off the rim of the tin pot she has balanced on her knees and drops to the floor. Before you could count to one, her foot slams down and kills it, leaving a thin green streak on the gray linoleum.

I'm sitting across from her, and I set my face on neutral so I don't add to her frustration by looking like a traitor. But if I let what's in my head come out, it would be *Yippee! Max is officially moving in. He makes Aunt Paulina happy. And you and I both know that is not an easy task.*

It's amazing the way she's changed since he came into her life and thawed out her heart. She treats *me* like a human being, and she even bought Nettie a new dryer so she doesn't have to freeze her fingers hanging clothes when it's below zero. And here's the whopper. She's stopped drinking so much and managed to get her driver's license back. The two years are up since she plowed over the fire hydrant in front of City Hall in the middle of the night. Nettie says the grapevine has it that Aunt Paulina kissed the police officer, offered him a swig of her bourbon, then passed dead out in his arms.

"Why don't you like him?" I ask. "He seems okay to me." I keep my eyes on the potato I'm peeling, and at first I think she's not going to answer.

"He's like a bloodsucker." She's done shucking, and now she's gathering the shells into a paper bag. "In fact, he's *worse* than a bloodsucker. *He* knows what he's doing." There's a strange kind of certainty in her voice that gets my attention and makes me stare at her hard. It's a warm summer day but not hot enough to make her face so red.

"What do you mean?" I don't know much about bloodsuckers, just that nobody wants anything to do with them.

She opens the cupboard under the sink and drops the bag of shells into the wastebasket. "He feeds off people, desperate women like your aunt."

Now I'm angry with her for making up stuff just because she doesn't like him. You'd think she'd be the last person in the world to judge someone without knowing all the facts. "I think he's nice. I'm glad he's coming." Well, there it is. She can do what she wants with it.

She puts her hand on my shoulder and pats it easy. "Just watch yourself, okay?"

I have no idea what she's talking about, but I give a lame "Uh-huh" so she'll get off the subject.

She swings me around in my chair so she's glaring straight into my eyes. "I *mean* it!" The words burst out of her mouth like they've broken down the door. "He's a shyster who came crawling out of the woodwork like a cockroach." She stands up straight, wipes her hands on her apron, and waits for me to say something.

I don't give her the satisfaction. I turn my back, grab another potato, and start peeling.

She clears her throat in a fake dramatic way. "Funny how he doesn't have a job. He just sits up there day after day in the new clothes she bought him, making her melt with his crazy love talk."

I keep peeling.

She shakes her head, then sighs like she's run out of steam. "Be careful, all right? I have a feeling he isn't here just for the queen's money." She cradles my chin in her hand and pulls my head against her stomach, then wraps both arms around it. "I think he has other things in mind."

Well, now I'm completely confused. If the other things she's hinting about mean me, she must be reading too many romance novels. And I am certainly not about to ask her to explain. There are *some* things you do not discuss with your grandmother. Besides, when a girl finally has a man who treats her like a daughter, she doesn't throw up her hands and say, *Oh, well, we don't have any proof, but maybe this one has a flaw. I'll just toss him away and wait for somebody better to come knocking on the door.*

"He doesn't have anything in mind," I say, "and I have to go get dressed."

Max and Aunt Paulina are taking me out for dinner and a movie in Burlington. It was Max's idea, my present for passing my grade. "Better late than never," he said at the dining-room table one morning. "Not everybody's kid brings home straight A's." While he was winking at me, I could see that Aunt Paulina was just dying to point out that he'd altered my C in math with a wide-tip pen. Instead, she just shook her head and finished eating her egg.

I'm in my room, putting on the new outfit Max talked Aunt Paulina into buying for the occasion—short denim skirt, pale blue halter, white sandals. My hair has grown back to shoulder length and I'm going to keep it this way. It's only been a week since I got my braces, and they've finally stopped beating up my mouth. I thought I would have to wait until I grew up and got a real job before I could have my teeth straightened. But Max took care of that. Aunt Paulina does anything he tells her to. He even talked her into buying me a whole new wardrobe, so my closet's filled to overflowing.

I am standing sideways in front of the mirror, inspecting my budding curves and my freshly shaven legs, which I managed to do with no nicks. I have finally become a full-fledged woman. A month ago, when the bleeding started, I wished so much that my mother could have been there to help me instead of Nettie. But I remembered what Mama told me. Everything happened like she said it would; only I didn't get the terrible cramps that are supposed to go along with the whole mess. I'm lucky in that respect. Beamer's pain is so bad that she has to stay in bed with a heating pad and a bottle of Midol for a whole day, sometimes two.

Aunt Paulina calls from down the hall to tell me they're ready. I hurry and put on a little lip gloss and a touch of blush blended in well to look natural.

"THIS IS MORE like it!" Max is driving the brand-new white Cadillac Aunt Paulina bought him. "I knew this baby'd behave for Papa," he says. He pounds the dashboard with his fist.

We've been speeding the whole way, and now he's blaring the horn and passing a worn-out pickup on a skinny, double-line road. Inside an old man is leaning forward, gripping the steering wheel and staring straight ahead. The woman in the passenger seat is scowling and waggling her finger at us.

"Goddamn Sunday drivers," Max yells out the window at nobody, because the truck is out of sight, as if this whale of a car ate it.

His behavior surprises me. I've never heard him swear before, and he always goes overboard to be nice to Nettie, never gets impatient with her slow-moving way. But then, maybe he's just excited about the new car and didn't really mean to lord it over those people. Everybody acts wrong once in a while.

"The water's beautiful today," Aunt Paulina says as we turn a corner and come face-to-face with Lake Champlain. "Maybe we could slow down so you could enjoy the view."

I see the muscles near his sideburns do a couple of push-ups before he takes his foot off the accelerator. "You got it, Paulie." He unbuckles her seat belt, pulls her toward him, and tucks her under his arm. "You're right. It'd be a shame to miss all this nice scenery."

Aunt Paulina smoothes down her hair and looks at the lake.

"We ought to get ourselves one of those," Max says. The way he is watching the water more than the road is putting me a little on edge.

"A sailboat?" There's a little excitement in Aunt Paulina's voice.

"Nah, those are for sissies. One of those high-powered jet boats. We could all go water-skiing."

Now that's something I could sell tickets for and make a bundle—her on a pair of water skis, getting her hair soaked.

"What do you think about that idea, Kat?" he calls back to me. "How'd you like to learn how to water ski? Your old uncle Max here's an expert. There's nothing to it."

"Sounds like fun." I can hear the falseness in my voice and wonder if he does. I've never told anyone how scared I am of the water. That my father thought it was a good idea to throw me off a dock because it would force me to learn how to swim. And how Mama paid a big price for fishing me out.

While they talk about which color speedboat to buy, I lean my head against the window and watch how the mountains are reflecting on the water. It reminds me of the photo on the postcard I sent Mr. Beck after I got his Empire State Building one.

"I don't know how to thank you, Katherine," he said the day we finished his manuscript. "This never would have been possible without you." He put his arm around my shoulder, and when I looked up to speak, I saw the tears, so I just smiled.

He cleared his throat and said, "We'll be back from New York in time for school. My agent's an old friend of mine, and he's invited us to stay at his apartment while he's at his summer home on Long Island. That way I can work with my editor and Johnny can have a change of scenery. God knows, he needs it."

Mr. Beck got a good chunk of money just for sending in part of the book. And now that it's finished, he'll get an even bigger chunk. Then when it's published, well, you can just imagine. So he's arranged to have the house painted inside and out, the lawn redone, and Mrs. Beck's roses replaced by the front porch. He gave me the key and asked me to be in charge of taking in the mail, watering the plants, and locking up after the workers leave. Walking around that empty house reminds me how much I miss Mr. Beck and Johnny and how glad I'll be when they get back.

WHEN WE GET to the movie theater, Max won't take no for an answer. "Of course you want popcorn, Kat. It's a rule. You go to a movie, you eat popcorn."

"But I'm stuffed. I can't eat another bite."

"That's no excuse. Besides, I'll help you with it. Paulie will, too. Won't you, hon?"

Aunt Paulina looks at Max with pain on her face. "I never want to see food again. I can't believe I let you talk me into having dessert after eating that whole lobster."

"We'll have a box of popcorn, some Raisinets, and a pack of Doublemint gum," Max tells the lady behind the candy counter.

Aunt Paulina opens her purse and hands the woman the money, then waits for her change. "If you two want to kill yourselves, be my guest," she says with a giggle in her voice. "Just keep that junk away from me."

"I'm going to sit between my two beautiful girls," Max says after he's chosen the row he wants. "There's not a man in this place that's as lucky as I am."

When we're settled, he puts his arm across the back of Aunt Paulina's seat and asks me to hold the goodies so we can share. As I dig into the popcorn, I think how lucky *I* am. A man like Max doesn't come along every day, no matter *what* Nettie says.

Twenty-Three

I'M IN THE BACKYARD, sitting on a lawn chair, reading *The Good Earth*, when Nettie comes to the screen door. "Your friend Bernadette just called," she says. "She wants you to go to her house."

"She does?"

"That's what she said."

This is strange because Beamer has a summer job, babysitting for Mrs. Porter's brand-new grandson. Her daughter lives five miles away, so mostly we just talk on the phone. Maybe she has today off.

"WAIT'LL YOU SEE what I have," Beamer says when she opens the door. "His name's Sam, and he's the cutest little person in the whole world." She grabs me by the hand and pulls me into the living room over to a portable crib in the corner. She uncovers him so tenderly, you'd think he was *her* baby.

He's lying on his stomach, and his legs are tucked in so tightly that his tiny behind is sticking straight up in the air. His hands are clenched into little fists as if he's trying to hold on to something important, and his body is moving to the beat of the breaths he's taking in. His head is covered with blond down and his skin is so thin, you can see little blue veins that look like strings traveling along underneath it.

"Well? What do you think?" Beamer's standing there with anticipation on her face so intense, it could be a live thing.

"He's adorable," I say. "But why's he here? You usually babysit at his house."

"Mrs. Porter's working downstairs, doing my mother's job. She wanted to spend some time with him, so she brought us over here." She smiles at Sam, then covers him back up. "He'll be awake soon. You can help me feed and change him."

I'd love to do that. He's so little, though, I think I'll just watch.

"Do you want to hold him?" Beamer asks, after she's fed Sam and changed his diaper.

"I don't think I'd better," I say. "I've never held a baby before." I hope she doesn't push this. I might break him.

"Then it's time you learned—and I have to pee, so sit on the couch and I'll hand him to you."

"Why don't you just put him in his little bed and I'll watch him there."

"This is his playtime," Beamer says like I should know that. "He doesn't want to go to bed."

"Oh, okay," I say. "Just a minute. Let me get ready." I sit down and hold out my arms stiff, as if she's about to load me up with wood.

She gives me an impatient look and does a little jiggle dance. "Relax. He's a baby, not a box of groceries. Just let your arms rest on your lap."

She sure did get to be an expert fast. "Okay, how's this?"

"Perfect. The only thing you have to remember is to support his head." She lays him in my lap and puts my hand in the proper place at the back of his neck. "Now I've really gotta go. He'll be fine. I'll be right back."

Well, now what am I supposed to do? I'll pat his hand. Oohh. He's got the most adorable little fingers with real miniature fingernails. Oh my gosh. He's wrapped his sweet little baby hand around my finger and he's squeezing—kind of an air squeeze, but I can feel it. Okay, now he's smiling at me. He definitely doesn't have any teeth, and I wonder if his mother knows that he has a blister on his upper lip. Yow! His eyes just did this really weird twirly thing. All right, now they're staying where they should be. They're sort of no color. A little bit navy blue. A little bit gray. But that's okay. They're kind of pretty. Maybe he'll be the only person in the world with this color of eyes. Well, now they're closed, and he's just lying there all limp.

"He fell asleep again?" Beamer's standing by the couch, smiling down at us.

"I guess he doesn't want to play after all."

She sits down next to me and touches the satiny hem of his blanket. "Weesie's coming home." She says the words the way you'd hold a robin's egg.

It takes me a second to understand. Then I nearly forget and almost let out a scream. Instead, I whisper, "Oh my god. That's great. What happened?"

"When she found out that my mother had lied to her and was planning to stay there, she threw a fit and wouldn't go to any of the auditions. She even threatened to hitchhike back here."

"What about your mother? Is she coming, too?"

At first she doesn't answer. "Nah. I don't think she'll ever come back."

"Is your father okay?" Well, that's a stupid question. Of course he's not okay. His wife left him.

"He'd never say so, but I think he's relieved that she's gone. He says you can't make somebody love you."

I think about what Mama went through. "He's right about that."

This baby is just the sweetest thing. He's actually sucking in his sleep. And he smells like angels must smell.

Beamer takes Sam, cradles him under her chin, and strokes his back. Then he wakes up again and lets out an ear-splitting burp, and we look at each other and laugh.

"How can somebody that small make such a huge noise?" I ask while Beamer rearranges him so he's lying on her legs, looking up at her.

"It scared the heck out of me the first time he did it, but before his mother went back to work, she spent a whole week teaching me how to take care of him, and she said it was normal." Okay, so that's why she knows everything.

Well, Sam can't make up his mind about what he wants to do. Now his face is all squinched up and red, and he's screaming his head off. Beamer stands up, balances him on her shoulder, and starts doing a little wiggle walk across the room. She's singing the "Hush, Little Baby" song. I walk over and pantomime that I'm leaving now. She nods and mouths, *Thanks for coming,* then goes back to her singing.

On my way to the door, Beamer calls, "When Weesie gets back, Sam's mom will be bringing him here every day so I can take care of Weesie, too. Come over anytime you want."

I smile and think how sometimes things just unfold in your favor and you don't know who to thank.

Twenty-Four

NETTIE'S GOING to move into Mr. Beck's house. He's rolling in money now, and she'll work for him when she's not busy here. The thought of us living right next door to each other makes me so happy, I feel like singing.

I'm folding laundry on the kitchen table while Nettie irons one of Max's shirts. The steam makes the mixture of bleach and spray starch come alive, and for a quick minute, I'm watching Mama do up my father's shirts with such tender care, you'd think they belonged to God. It's funny how a fragrance can be so powerful that it carries you back to a whole different time and place. And the fact that I can finally think about Mama without having my heart shut down makes me feel a little bit guilty. But time has brought a weird kind of peace to the whole thing. People said it would happen. Now I believe them.

"I'm glad Aunt Paulina agreed to let you take the job," I say.

"She didn't have much choice," Nettie replies. Her voice has a tone of confidence that I've never heard before when she's spoken about Aunt Paulina.

"What do you mean?"

"She's been threatening to fire me since you found out who I am. She kept saying that nobody else would hire me and I believed her. Then Mr. Beck called and offered me room and board and a wonderful salary to boot. It took the wind right out of her sails, but she wasn't about to match his offer. She's always loved the fact that I was barely making ends meet and that she could order me around like a slave."

I smile. "Well, now she can't."

She shakes her head and smiles, too. "Nope. Not anymore."

"When are you moving?" I ask. I hate folding Aunt Paulina's underwear. She could at least do that herself. She just wanders around the house, doing nothing except telling Nettie and me what to do.

"I told Mr. Beck I'd be there this afternoon."

"I'll help you." I'm so glad she won't be living in that horrible old rooming house another day.

"Thanks," she says, "I can use the help." She shoves a chunk of defiant hair behind her ear, grabs the last shirt from the basket, and slams it onto the ironing board. "We can do that as soon as I'm finished with this." She adds a twist of lemon to the word *this* as if that shirt is Max himself. "That'll give me time to get their dinner in the oven before I have to get back here."

"WHERE DO YOU want this?" I'm holding Nettie's hot plate and wondering why the frayed cord hasn't electrocuted her. We're in the Becks' spare room, unpacking the last of her boxes. Mr. Beck's at the barbershop and Johnny's just outside the door, watching Nettie's every move. He's not swaying back and forth or making the high-pitched sound he usually makes when he's nervous. When Nettie asked if he wanted to help, he didn't run to his room and slam the door. He just stood there with his plain face, no fear at all.

"You can put it on the bed for now," she says. "I'll store it someplace up in the closet."

"I'll do it!" Johnny bounds into the room, takes the hot plate out of my hands, and puts it on the top closet shelf. He stands back and beams at Nettie. "I did it good?"

She pats his arm. "You did it just right."

Johnny rubs his hands together, then says in an excited voice, "Okay. Okay. Now what?"

Instead of telling him there's nothing more to do like *I* was about to, she slides her suitcase out from under the bed. "Well, now," she says, drumming her fingers along her chin. "Let's see. I wonder where we should put this. How about behind that bookcase next to the window?"

"How about here? There's room right here." Johnny grabs the tray of knickknacks from the bureau, puts it on the floor, and plops the suitcase on the embroidered dresser scarf Nettie's mother made. "Is that just right, too?"

Nettie swallows hard. "That's perfect. I don't know why *I* didn't think of that."

"And is this perfect, too?" He places the tray on top of the suitcase and makes sure it's centered.

"Couldn't be better," Nettie says, smiling.

"And it's perfect, too?"

"It's perfect, too."

There is a talent some people have when they are around a person with a need. And I'm watching it pour out of Nettie like a waterfall. But then, I guess she has a need, too. Now maybe she'll get the respect and appreciation she deserves. I just wish I could move here with her.

NETTIE AND I are sitting outside the barbershop in Mr. Beck's car, waiting for Johnny to have his hair cut.

I roll the window down, think how hot it is for September, and wonder if I should ask the question I've been dying to ask since I moved here. I was hoping she'd tell me on her own, but she never did. And I guess this is as good a time as any. "Why doesn't Aunt Paulina like you?" I say in a cautious voice. "What did you ever do to her?"

I guess I've stepped over the line. There's a big awkward silence, and just as I'm about to apologize for being nosy, she says, "She blames me for messing up your father's life. She said I should have stepped in and objected when he told me he was going to marry your mother. If I'd done that, he would have come to his senses and married Paulina. She says that she could have made him happy. And, well . . . she blames me for everything that happened to Jacob, even his death."

I take another step. "If she hates you so much, why did she hire you?"

"To punish me. To make me pay for ruining her life. She knew I wanted to be near you, so she did everything she could think of to torment me. The thing is, she doesn't really bother me. God knows I've put up with a lot worse than her."

"But you're still going to work at our house when you're not busy at the Becks'," I say. "Why doesn't she just hire somebody new?"

She inhales deeply, then takes her time letting the air

out. "Let's just say she doesn't want everyone to know her business. Her last maid was with her parents forever and was like part of the family. And she knows I'd never bad-mouth her because she's your aunt."

"Well, you've got her now." This explains why Aunt Paulina's been in such a rotten mood lately.

"Yep," she says, the drawling cowboy way. "Guess it's my turn."

But there's still something else on my mind. "Why do all that extra work? You've got everything you need at the Becks'. You could just stay over there, away from her."

Her face changes to serious. "I need to be with you. If I couldn't, I wouldn't have taken the job."

I kind of knew that already, but I just wanted to hear her say it. I smile and give her a peck on the cheek. "I need to be with you, too."

Mr. Beck and Johnny are coming out of the barbershop. "There they are," I say. "I'm going to go help Mr. Beck."

When Johnny's settled in the backseat with me, he taps Nettie on the shoulder and grins huge. "I look good, Nana?"

Nettie turns around, then pauses. "You look very good, Johnny, but I'm not . . ."

Mr. Beck clears his throat and nods his head.

"You look handsome, Johnny, just like a movie actor," Nettie says, in a voice that reminds me of sunshine.

I think of all the years Nettie wasn't able to be with her son and now she has Johnny. Maybe it's time I made friends with God again. I've kind of missed him. I say a quick little thank-you prayer. And you have to hand it to God. Some days he just outdoes himself.

Twenty-Five

I AM FINALLY in high school. If you mess up here, you will have four years to regret it. If you do everything right, you will get a lot of nice comments in your senior yearbook and maybe a friendship or two that will last forever. But the first thing you have to do is learn how to work the stubborn combination to your locker. It's been a week and it's still fighting with me and winning.

"Need help with that?" A thin, dark-haired boy is taking a notebook out of the locker next to mine. He's being polite by not staring while I struggle to work the lock with one hand and juggle a mountain of books with the other.

"That's okay. I think I can get it." This boy is not the movie-star, quarterback type, but a nip at my gut makes me smooth down my hair and run my tongue along the corners of my mouth. You can't trust spit to stay where it belongs.

"Here, why don't you let me give it a try." He takes my books and puts them on the floor. "What's your combination?"

"Thirty-two, eleven, thirteen." I have recited those numbers so many times, I will still remember them when my head is empty and I'm living in an old-age home.

I should back up to give him room, but I don't. My feet are stuck to the tile like they are saying, *I don't care. I'm not moving.* I smell his clean boy scent. His light blue shirt matches his eyes perfectly, and his jeans fall just right over his flat butt. My heart is saying, *Yes, please.*

He says, "Well, it works."

For a minute I forgot what he was doing, and I'm surprised to see the open locker. "Voilà!" Oh god. I can't believe I just said that. It shows on his face. He thinks I'm a moron.

"I see Mademoiselle Bousquet's taught you her favorite word already," he says, smiling. His teeth are so white and he has perfect lips. "I've got her for French II. She's the best."

He's a *sophomore.* I should have known. He's way too mature to be a freshman. "Right," I say. What's the matter with me? I used to be able to talk to people and make sense.

"Do you want to try?"

"Try what?" Oh, try opening the locker. What else could he mean? He's standing there, pointing at it. "Sure."

We do that little dance thing where you both go in the same direction at once. He laughs, puts his hands on my arms, turns me toward the locker, and stands next to me.

"Start by spinning the lock to the right a few times." He reaches over to demonstrate. His breath smells like pineapple juice. I *love* pineapple juice. "Now back up to the thirty-two line."

My hand is shaking so badly that I go way past the number. He spins the knob again, then puts his hand over mine and guides it to the right place. Now the deepest, most private part of me is doing calisthenics. How's a girl supposed to concentrate on these stupid little lines when all she wants to do is wrap her arms around this boy and kiss him silly? "Okay, there. I think I got it."

"Good. Now we'll head for the eleven. We'll just take our time." Wait a minute. Is his hand shaking, too? I think it is. "By the way," he says in his just-right voice, "I'm David Weston." Of course his name is David. It's my favorite name in the whole world. It's the name I've picked for my first baby boy.

"I'm Kat. I mean Katherine Farrington."

"I know," he says. He knows. Oh my lord. He knows

my name. But how? "I asked my father. He's your algebra teacher."

Well, sometimes God just has it in for you. I picture the lottery guy taking my prize back. He was just kidding about me being the big winner. And now the arrow on the lock is pointing to thirteen. What else would it be pointing to? Mr. Weston's the meanest teacher in the entire universe. I think he just crawled out of hell. Plus, he thinks I'm a complete idiot. Math was bad enough when there were just numbers to worry about. Now they've thrown in letters to confuse you even more. "Oh" is all I can manage.

David must see my shoulders collapse because he says, "He's really not that bad. He used to be a marine, so he uses the boot-camp technique for the first couple weeks. But after that . . . well . . . he's not such a bad guy. You'll see."

"It's just that I'm not very good in math. It's like that part of my brain doesn't work." Okay, now *he* thinks I'm a simpleton and he'll be polite, but he'll leave and that'll be the end of it.

"I can help you with it, if you want. Math's kind of my best subject."

Just when I thought it was going to rain, the sun comes out. "Great! I'd like that."

"You do know you just opened your locker, right?"

Well, what do you know. I won't have to carry my books around the whole day. "Thanks for the help."

"No problem. I gotta run. Catch you later."

"Yeah, okay. Later." Sometimes I'm such a bonehead. A popular girl would have said something clever.

"Hey, Kat!" He's turned around, walking backward.

"Yes?"

"You have lunch fifth period, right?"

"Right." A little thrill runs through me because he even knows when I eat.

"Me, too. Okay if I save you a place?"

"If you want to." Oh boy, I sure hope he wants to.

"I want to." He smiles.

I smile back. Sometimes, when you wake up in the morning, it's just plain old Tuesday. But things sure can change in a hurry.

On my way to English, I run into Beamer. She's wearing one of the new outfits she bought with her babysitting money. Her hair is fastened up in back with the leather spiky thing she found in a mall in Burlington the day her father took us shopping. And she's wearing just enough makeup to highlight her features. She doesn't let on that she sees a cute guy eyeing her as he goes by.

"You're not going to believe this," I say, pulling her to the side of the hall.

"Believe what?"

I tell her about David and how he asked me to meet him at lunch.

"Wow!" she says. "That's great. He sounds fantastic." She looks at her watch. "I've got to go. I have Mr. Weston next and I'll get detention if I'm late." As she turns to leave, she says, "Meet me by the front door after school so I can hear all the details about David."

Right. Like his last name.

As I watch her walk away, I think how much she's changed and it makes me glad. I think she was like a flower trying to bloom the whole time, but her mother's foot was holding her down. Now she can grow the way she's supposed to.

I'm NOT SURE what to do when I get to the cafeteria. Usually, I sit at an anonymous table with other girls who don't know anybody, either.

Today I stand by the door, thinking that David was just teasing me, when I see him running toward me, waving. "Sorry," he says, out of breath, "Coach made me stay after to do laps because I'm useless in gym. He thinks it'll toughen me up."

Well, this is a little uncomfortable. Him telling me something embarrassing like that. We're the same height, so I can see straight into his eyes. Nothing, not the least bit of anger. "Doesn't that bother you? Being picked on like that?"

"Nah. He's a miserable old coot. It makes him feel better, and I'm happy to help. Let's go eat. I'm starving."

I'm sitting in Mademoiselle Bousquet's class. She's so classy. I wonder why she's teaching a bunch of kids French when she could be in Paris, sipping wine in a little café with *un homme.* While she's writing verbs on the board, I'm thinking how easy David is to talk to and how we've eaten lunch together every day for a month. It's going to be so exciting to go to the fall formal with him. "We'll double-date," he said right after I said yes. "My friend Jack's a senior. He has a car."

"Sounds like fun," I said. It sounds like more than fun. At last my life is headed toward the good stuff.

Twenty-Six

WHEN THE DOORBELL rings, I'm waiting in the upstairs hall for Aunt Paulina to give me my cue. "A lady never appears anxious" was the first rule she listed while she was sitting on my bed *watching* me get dressed. "She makes the gentleman wait, so he'll appreciate her more."

Yeah, *right.* Just like she made Max wait to crawl into her bed—about two seconds.

"You must be David," I hear Aunt Paulina say in her high-and-mighty voice. "I'm Katherine's aunt. Come in and sit down. She'll be ready soon."

Oh lord. She's making him sit down. I picture her poised on the couch with her legs crossed at the ankle, her hands clasped on her lap, her face all pompous. I bet he's sorry he got into this mess. I wonder what she's going to ask him.

"So, David," she says. "What grade are you in?"

What grade?! I *told* her he's a sophomore.

"Tenth. I'm in the tenth grade."

Thank god he didn't call her ma'am. She hates that, thinks it makes her sound old.

"Katherine told me your father is her arithmetic teacher."

Arithmetic! For crying out loud. Didn't she ever go to high school?

"Yes, ma'am, he is."

There's a long stretch of silence. I lean against the wall and close my eyes. That did it. She's done with him. She'll call me down now and we can get out of here; he's not worth the wait.

"And what about your mother? Does she work, too?"

"She does work, but she works at home. She's an artist. In fact, you've got one of her oils right over there. The one above the piano."

Oh my gosh! Aunt Paulina loves the snow-covered mountains with the stream and the white birches in the foreground. She's always going on about how it cost more than all her other paintings combined.

She laughs deep in her throat, and I'm sure she's

giving David her pity look, the one where the skin between her eyes gets all bleached out and hilly. "Isabelle McIntyre did that painting," she says, with a *Boy, are you stupid* tone in her voice. "She's a famous artist. Not from around here, of course. Chicago, I think." I bet Aunt Paulina has grown a foot because of her straight back and stretched out neck. "But it's nice that your mother paints, too. It's good to have a hobby."

"You're right about Chicago," David says. His voice is perfect, medium low. "We lived there until a year ago. We moved here so my mother could be close to nature. And McIntyre's her maiden name. She's always signed with it."

Nothing from her. I suppose it's hard to talk when your jaw's sitting on your lap. I hear the back door slam and then Max's loud voice. "Paulie! I got some champagne to celebrate our little girl's first date. I'll stick it in the fridge." I guess this is what you call getting blasted with both barrels. I look for a hole I can fall into. "Oh, hi there," Max says when he gets to the living room. "I didn't know anybody was here. I'm Max, Kat's soon-to-be uncle. You must be David. Nice to meet you."

"Nice to meet you, too, sir." He's still there. I can't imagine why.

"Hey, Kat! Your date's here. You ready?" I guess Max doesn't know the make-him-wait rule.

I've been ready for an hour. "I'm coming," I say, on the

way down the stairs. "Hi, David." I am so nervous, my whole body is shaking.

David stands up and walks over to me. "Wow, Kat, you look really . . . Wow!" He says this out loud.

I grab my real thoughts by the collar and shove them to the back of my head. *You look so yummy and you smell so good.* "Thanks. You look nice, too."

He hands me a white box. I wasn't expecting a present, so I stand here like a dope until Aunt Paulina jumps in. "Well, Katherine, aren't you going to open your corsage?"

She forgot about this part of the lesson, so I'm on my own. As I lift the nest of lilies of the valley out of the box, it's as if Mama is standing right next to me, holding my hand, and telling me to smell their sweet scent. A lump fills my throat when I think how she used to talk about my first date and how exciting it would be for both of us. She even taught me how to dance. So now she's here, too. This is where you have to believe in fate. Just think of all the flowers he had to choose from. "They're beautiful, David, thank you."

"I don't know much about flowers," he says, shrugging his shoulders. "So my mother picked them out. They're her favorite." Now fate is stamping its foot to make sure it's got my attention.

Aunt Paulina takes the corsage and says to David, "Would you like to pin it on, or do you want me to?"

David glances at my strapless top, then down at the corsage, then back at me. "You should do it," he says fast. He looks so cute with his cheeks all pink. And I think how Mama would never have allowed me to wear anything like this. I'd probably have to be married first.

"What's your favorite flower?" I ask Aunt Paulina while she's struggling to get the pin through the thick burgundy taffeta of the dress Max picked out and she paid so much for that, I thought the price tag was a joke. But I like the way I look in this dress. It makes me feel a little bit like a movie star.

"Gardenias. I've always loved them. They're so rich and creamy. And their scent is so powerful. They put all the other flowers to shame."

I guess I should have known that's the one she'd choose. Mama hated them more than any other flower. She used to say they reminded her of death.

Max is holding the new camera Aunt Paulina gave him for his birthday. "Okay," he says, "now I'll take a couple of pictures, and then we'll let you two loose."

THE PERSON WHO invented slow dancing was a genius. It makes hugging right out in the open respectable. As long as the music keeps playing, go ahead, nobody thinks anything of it. Of course, between songs you have to let go, or you'll probably be asked to leave the dance.

David's holding me close, and we're swaying in time to the music. We are a perfect fit. Now, he's not what you'd call a good dancer. I'm doing most of the leading. But, boy, is it fun to have my chin resting on his shoulder and his cheek pressed against mine.

The slow song ends and the beat picks up. "How about we sit this one out," David says. He hasn't confessed that he doesn't know how to fast dance, but every time one comes on, we head for the bleachers or the punch bowl, which is okay with me. If he asked me to jump in a garbage truck and ride to the dump, I'd say I'd love to and mean it. I'm not sure if you believe in love at first sight, but I know I do.

THE PORCH LIGHT is on, but the rest of the house is dark. I thought Aunt Paulina would wait up to make sure I got home on time. David walks me to the door, and I wonder if I'll get to use the kissing lesson Beamer gave me.

"Just flatten your thumb along the side of your first finger and then let it relax a little," she said, demonstrating with her own hand. "See, it looks kind of like a mouth, a tiny bit open."

She was right, it did. "So now what do I do?"

"Just practice. Like this." She kissed her hand a few times. She looked like an expert, but why wouldn't she? "Okay, now you try."

I did. "How's that?" I thought I did it pretty well.

"You're kidding, right?"

"What'd I do wrong?"

"First of all, you don't shape your mouth into an O like a three-year-old. You let it go loose and keep it open just a little. Go ahead. Let me see. That's right. Now aim for the upper lip."

"You mean the upper finger."

"All right, smart-ass. The upper finger. Just do it."

I did an excellent job. "Better?"

She opened her eyes huge and shook her head as if I were the biggest idiot she'd ever known. "It's only better if David enjoys kissing a dead goldfish. You have to clamp on and put some passion into it. Here, give me your hand. I'll show you what I mean."

While she was making out with my fingers, I thought about what Aunt Paulina said. "A well-brought-up young lady never lets the boy kiss her on the first date. He'll think you're easy, and you could get yourself into a real mess. Besides, he'll like you better if you give him a challenge, make him earn your affection."

David's already earned my affection, and while we're standing under the porch light, I'm hoping he likes girls who kiss on the first date. "Would you like to go to the movies next Friday?" he asks. There's a little nervousness in his voice as if he actually thinks I might say no.

"I'd love to." I'm not going to ask what the movie is because I don't care. But I can't think of anything else to say. "What's playing?"

He smiles and shrugs his shoulders. "I have no idea. Does it matter?"

"Not to me."

"Not to me, either."

I laugh and change feet a few times. *Please, God. Let him kiss me now.*

"Kat?"

"Yes?"

"Is it okay if I kiss you?"

"I'd like that." All right, here goes, but I can't remember one thing Beamer told me. I am going to mess this up so bad.

David puts his hands on my shoulders, touches his lips to mine, and stays just long enough for boiling water to race through my body. "I've never kissed a girl before," he says in a shy voice. "I'm not very good at it."

Well, look at this. We're both brand-new. Nobody else's fingerprints on either one of us. "I think you're really good at it."

The porch light flickers and breaks the mood. He says, "I guess I should go."

The end so soon. This is always the way with good things. "Yeah, I guess."

He puts his hands in his pockets. "Well, good night. I had a really nice time."

I am so filled with longing that my words come out in a whisper. "I had a nice time, too."

There's no moon, and the dark devours him like he was just a dream. I can't wait to get to my room. I'll lie on my bed, relive the whole wonderful night a thousand times in my head, and think about next Friday.

I go into the living room, turn on the light, and head for the kitchen to get a Pepsi. "Have a good time?" Max is sitting on the couch, smoking a cigarette. His voice is low and raspy like the soap opera men Nettie watches on TV, and it startles me. I didn't see him there. Why was he sitting in the dark? "How'd everything go?"

"Fine. It went fine. Where's Aunt Paulina?"

He drops his cigarette into the empty champagne bottle on the coffee table. That's when I notice there's only one glass beside it. "She drank the whole bottle and went to bed early. In fact, she's passed dead out. So I decided to wait up for you."

"But she's not supposed to drink," I say. "She hasn't had anything for months. I thought you bought the champagne for yourself." Until tonight he's been helping her stay sober.

"This was a special occasion," he says. "Once isn't going to hurt anything. She'll be fine tomorrow." He can't possibly believe that. Why would he ruin it?

He pats the couch next to him. "Come tell me all about the dance."

I don't think so. Sometimes you just know to get out of a place. "I'm going to bed. I'll tell you all about it to-morrow." I start for the back stairs.

He jumps up and grabs my arm. "Hey, slow down. You owe me."

"Owe you for what?"

"The dress. Paulie would never have spent that much if I hadn't talked her into it."

"You're hurting me," I say, trying to wriggle out of his grasp. "I'm tired. I really just want to lie down."

He shoves me onto the couch, sits on the edge, and digs his hand into my shoulder. "How's that?"

"Please, Max, let me go." This can't be happening.

He runs his fingers through my hair, down my cheek, then over my lips. "He's not much of a kisser, is he, the little pissant? He pecked at you like he was kissing his mother for christ's sake."

Help me, God. Please *help me.*

"You're dressed like a woman, Katherine. And I'm going to show you what it feels like to be with a man." He lowers his face toward mine.

I stop breathing. *God, can't you hear me? Are you even there?*

He covers my mouth with his. Thick, putrid saliva mixes with mine. I taste bile rising in my throat and wish

I could throw up. My mind leads me away from this place, and we go looking for my mother. When we find her, she's wearing her pink funeral suit, but I can't see her face. Her hands are covering her eyes and she's crying. *Mama, I need you. Please help me. Mama!*

Then everything stops and I hear Nettie's voice, slow and serious. "If you don't get out of here, so help me God, I'll kill you." She's holding a butcher knife against his neck.

"I'll go," he says, not moving. "Just put that thing down." He slides off the couch and grabs the knife from Nettie. He glares at her, opens his mouth, and starts to say something. But then he closes it again and drops the knife to the floor. He goes over to the closet, gets his coat, and walks out the front door. He leaves without saying a word, doesn't even look back.

I FILL THE BATHTUB with water as hot as I can stand and sit here shivering. "How did you know?" I ask. Nettie's washing me gently, like I'm her little girl.

"I *didn't* know. I thought they'd gone to bed, so I waited up for you and watched for the light to go on. I wanted to see you in your dress and hear all about your special night, just us." She looks away. "Then when I got here . . ."

I'm all tight inside, the way I felt when my mother told me she was going to die. I guess something this big is too much for a brain to handle all at once, so it tells the body to shut down and only let a little of the bad in at a time. "Where will he go? He didn't take any of his stuff."

"He'll go on to his next victim." She opens the hamper and drops the washcloth into it. "And you've seen the stash of money he keeps in his wallet. He can live in fine style for a long time." She helps me out of the tub, wraps a towel around me, and hands me one for my hair.

"But how do we know he won't come back?"

"She won't let him. She's not *that* crazy. At least I don't think she is. Besides, men like him have pasts they don't want dredged up. If we went to the police, women would come crawling out of cracks from miles around to get revenge."

"The police! I don't want to go to the police. I don't want anyone to know about this. I'd die before I told anybody what he did to me."

She hands me a nightie. I put it back and get Mama's from the bottom of the pile. I haven't worn it since the night I got here, but tonight I need it. Nettie nods, seems to understand, and helps me into it. Then she starts wringing her hands and looks at me with concerned eyes. I am a crisis. "I have to go over to the Becks' to leave a note and turn out the lights," she says. "I'll just be a minute. Will you be all right alone?"

I nod and get into bed. I try not to let the bad thoughts

come to the surface. I lock them away in the blackest corner of my mind, but they keep forcing their way back out. I think how a few minutes ago, I was David's girl, clean and new. Now I'm covered with Max's filthy finger-prints, and all the soap in the world won't wash them away.

When Nettie comes back into the room, I pretend I'm asleep. I'm just too tired to talk anymore. I hear a jingling noise next to me and then she goes around and crawls in on the other side of the bed. Just before she reaches over me to turn out the light, I open my eyes and see Max's keys to the house and his car on the nightstand. The silver key ring with his initials in script is the last thing I see before the darkness comes. It's comforting to know that he can't get into the house. But with a person, you don't need a key. You just break in and kill their soul.

I'M IN THE upstairs hall, listening to loud voices coming from the kitchen.

"What are you *talking* about? He'd *never* do anything like that."

"He would have done *more* than that if I hadn't gotten here when I did."

"You're making this up. You never liked him. You couldn't stand the fact that I was finally happy and that you never will be."

I go down the back stairs and look Aunt Paulina in the eye. "She's telling the truth."

Her face loses its rage and she lowers her voice. "But he thought of you as a daughter." She shakes her head and starts gasping for air. "This is all a mistake. He's affectionate, that's all. You just took it wrong."

"I didn't take it wrong."

She puts her coffee cup down, leans against the counter, and crosses her arms. "Well then, you must have done something to lead him on. What did you do?"

"I didn't do anything. I just tried to get away."

"Why didn't you scream? I would have heard you."

I glance over at the sink where Nettie put the champagne bottle.

Aunt Paulina's body sags. She drops the bottle into the trash and goes back upstairs.

The quiet is worse than the yelling, and I know she's not finished with me yet.

Twenty-Seven

MR. BECK IS letting me use Mrs. Beck's sewing machine to alter Mama's clothes. She left a good hem and generous seams on purpose. The depth of her love and the hugeness of the loss are back in full force. It's as if God didn't get my whole soul the first time, so now he's gone back in to take the rest.

"Want some?" Johnny's standing next to me, holding a glass of chocolate milk.

No, I don't want anything. I'll never want anything ever again. "Sure. Thanks." I take the milk, smile, and try to make it look genuine.

"Can I watch?" Before I have a chance to answer, he

pulls a straight-back chair over to the sewing machine and sits down so close that our elbows are touching. "What are you doing? Sewing?"

"Yes."

"Why?"

"I need some new clothes."

"Why?"

Oh, I just want to be with my own self. And Johnny takes so much extra. But you have to find it, because he's like a newborn puppy with big demands. "I have to have new ones because my other ones are gone."

"Gone where?" He leans forward and looks me straight in the face.

Nettie drove me to the Salvation Army and helped me carry in the clothes Aunt Paulina bought me. "I gave them to another girl."

"Is that why your eyes are sad?" His hands are folded between his knees, and he's rocking back and forth.

I must have taken my foot off the pedal, because the whirring noise stops and a fierce silence falls over the room. Then, as if his words have reached in and squeezed the sad part of my heart, tears come and drop onto the blue fabric of my sleeve.

Johnny's face freezes and his words come out with a moan. "Oh . . . oh . . . look what I did." He jumps up and pushes his chair back with such force that it nearly tips over. He starts for the door but stops. Then he comes back and reaches into the neck of his shirt. He lowers the string with Mama's ring over my head. "This will make your face smile." He pats my shoulder with his straight-out hand and then he's gone.

Something inside me fills up when I hold the ring in my closed fist, then rub it against my cheek. This ring held a family together—one that was raggedy on the edges and had parts that were knife-blade sharp, but it was mine. And the daddy of that family would have killed the person who made his daughter feel so dirty that she wants to kill herself but doesn't know how.

Twenty-Eight

"THERE HAS TO BE *something* the matter," Beamer says. "You're acting like somebody died." We're in her living room, sitting on the couch.

"I told you. Nothing's wrong."

"Are you feeling okay? You look terrible."

I *feel* terrible. My stomach is sick and there's a deep ache where my heart used to be. "I'm fine."

"Well, you look awful. Your hair's a mess and your face is all splotchy. And why are you wearing that old dress?"

"My mother made it. I like it."

She looks down. "Oh. Sorry. I didn't know."

"That's okay."

"Well then, what is it?"

"It's nothing." I rearrange my face. "Look, I'm smiling. Now can we change the subject?"

"Did David do something? He seems like such a nice guy."

I go back the porch, to the gentleness of David's mouth on mine—his sweet breath and tender arms.

"It wasn't David. David's perfect." I feel so awful, like I've got the flu, only worse because my cozy inside is gone, replaced by gloom. I can't imagine ever feeling sunshiny again. And only yesterday I felt happiness bigger than anything. I have to tell her. I'm going to die if I don't.

"What is it, then?" She looks scared.

"It was Max. He tried to . . . I don't know . . . He was all over me."

"Oh my god!" She looks at me with frantic eyes. "But I thought he was nice. You've told me a million times how much you like him."

"I did like him."

"What do you think made him change so fast?"

"I don't know. It must have been the dress. I shouldn't have worn a dress like that."

"That's crazy."

"Well, he never acted like that when I was in regular clothes. It had to have been the dress, so it's my fault."

She grabs hold of my arms and shakes me a little. "You have to stop talking like this and go tell your aunt."

"She already knows."

"What did she say?"

"She doesn't believe me."

"Oh shit, Kat. What're you going to do? You can't go back there."

"He's gone."

"Your aunt threw him out?"

I tell her about Nettie.

"Good for her."

"I don't want to talk about this anymore," I say. "It makes me feel worse."

"Would it help if we went to church?"

"What?"

"You know. Go see your priest."

"I don't have a priest." I don't even have a preacher. Not here. That was part of my old life with Mama.

"We could go see mine."

"We could?"

"Sure. You could even go to confession, if that would help."

"I don't think I'm allowed, am I? Don't you have to be Catholic?"

"You're supposed to be, but who's gonna know? I'll go in first and tell him you're my cousin from out of town."

"You're going to lie to a priest?"

"If it'll make *you* feel better. He's used to me having a lot more to confess than a little fib."

I don't know about this. "Do they have to keep what you say a secret?"

"Yes. Even if you kill somebody. They can't tell a soul."

"And after you say what you did wrong, you're forgiven?"

"That's the way it works."

Anything's worth a try. "Okay, what do I have to do?"

MY HANDS ARE folded in my lap. I have my eyes smashed closed like in the doctor's office when you're about to get a shot. "Bless me, Father, for I have sinned. It's been a long time since my last confession."

"How long?" Beamer said he was old. He doesn't sound old. Maybe I got the wrong one.

"Very long."

"How long is very long?"

I guess I can't slide by this one. "Never."

"Are you a Catholic, child?" Here goes. He's going to kick me out. I wonder if you can be arrested for something like this.

"No. I'm . . . um . . . kind of a Nazarene. But not since I moved here."

"And how can I help?"

"I did something wrong."

"Do you want to tell me about it?"

No, I don't want to tell anybody about it. "I guess."

"Go ahead, I'm listening."

Max's tongue in my mouth. His hands all over me. His disgusting breath. I should have fought harder. Why didn't I fight harder?

"Did you take the Lord's name in vain?"

What? Oh. "No."

"Did you lie to your parents?"

"No."

"Steal something?"

"No."

"Did you do something with a boyfriend? Something you regret?"

"No." I don't regret anything I did with David. Just that I won't be able to do anything with him ever again. He deserves so much better than me.

"Well then, what is it? I can't help you if you don't tell me." His voice is saying, *Let's go!*

"I wore the wrong dress." That has to be what it was. If I'd worn the kind of dress Mama would have wanted me to, nothing would have happened. It's all my fault.

"The wrong dress?"

"Yes. I should have worn a different dress."

"Child, are you feeling all right?"

"No. I feel terrible."

"Maybe you should talk to your mother about this."

"That's a good idea. I shouldn't have bothered you."
What was I thinking?

"No bother. Go in peace."

I look over to thank him for his time, but the little door is already closed. I should have known by now that God always gets the last word. He doesn't give second chances. When you do something bad, you can't say, *Wait . . . wait just a minute! I made a mistake. Let me go back. I'll do the right thing this time.* It doesn't work that way—not even if you're just a kid.

He keeps you dangling like a fish caught on the end of a line. You have the tiniest bit of hope that you can still wiggle your way back into the murky river of your life and hide your guilt behind a rock—but you can't.

Twenty-Nine

"I'LL BE GOING out in a little while. I probably won't get back until late." This is the first real thing Aunt Paulina's said to me since that day in the kitchen, and here it is almost Christmas. We've settled into a solemn existence that is beginning to feel normal, not bad. It's about the same as it was when I first got here. Mainly we ignore each other and the weeks pass.

When I'm not in school, I spend most of my time with Beamer or at the Becks'. And Nettie and I have returned to our cozy meals in the kitchen while Aunt Paulina eats in the dining room and then goes back upstairs.

For once, I don't blame Aunt Paulina for my misery.

Max fooled her the same as he did me. But I don't think she'll ever get over the fact that I was the reason he left, just like my mama was the reason my daddy left.

Tonight Nettie went home early, and I'm standing at the sink, washing the supper dishes. "The radio announcer just said it's going to sleet." I don't expect a reply. It was just something to say.

"They'll sand the roads."

Well, I *know* that. "Right. It just said to be careful."

"I will." She's acting all nervous, like I'm not going to let her go or something. Now she's checking the refrigerator for the third time. It's filled to overflowing. She went grocery shopping this afternoon, and it took Nettie and me forever to get the stuff in from the car and put away. "You'd think she was having the president over for Christmas dinner," Nettie said while she was putting T-bone steaks in the freezer.

"Do you know if Nettie put clean sheets on my bed today?" Aunt Paulina says. "I told her to, but I forgot to ask if she did." She's drying a plate. This is strange because she never does housework. And she's all dressed up with makeup on. Since Max left, she's stayed mostly in her bathrobe and usually in her room. Things don't generally change this fast.

"I saw her take a load of laundry downstairs," I say. There's a little drum beating in the back of my head. It started out slow and now it's going faster. And I don't know why I'm suddenly out of breath.

"Well then," she says. "I'm going to go check my bathroom and make sure it's clean."

Why would she need to check her bathroom? It's always clean. *Oh.* Now I see. As soon as she leaves, I'll go to the Becks'. The drum is going crazy. I finish the dishes without really drying them, then go to my room and try to read a chapter of *Ethan Frome.*

My door opens slowly. "I'm leaving now." Her voice is soft-sweet, wrong for her.

"Okay." I don't look up.

If you know Starkfield, Massachusetts, you know the post-office.

"Katherine, I'm going to pick up Max. He's coming back."

I already figured that out.

If you know the post-office you must have seen Ethan Frome drive up to it . . .

I'm cold all of a sudden. My teeth are chattering so hard, I think they might break.

"He told me what happened," she says. "About the misunderstanding. He wants to talk to you about it when he gets here. Everything's going to be fine. You'll see. He's not angry. He's anxious to see you. He wants us to be a family again."

There was something bleak and unapproachable in his face, and he was so stiffened and grizzled that I took him for an old man and was surprised to hear that he was not more than fifty-two.

"He'll do it again," I say. The words come out as somber as the thought. I stare her straight in the eyes and watch her draw back just a little.

"That's a lie," she yells. "He never did anything to you."

"He tried to rape me. Nettie saw him. We'll go to the police and tell them what he did."

Her face drops. She doesn't say anything.

"They'll arrest him and throw him in jail."

The wild air of the storm that's surrounding her picks up speed, and her brassy voice cuts through the room like a sword. "Do you think for one minute that they'll believe her?" she says. "She's a murderer for god's sake. I'll tell them that she's been stealing from me and they'll arrest *her.*"

I try to get her to look at me. She won't. "Don't you even care what kind of person he is?"

She waits so long to answer that I think she's actually reconsidering. "If he did anything to you, it's because you asked for it. Look at what your mother did. You're just like her. Whatever you got, you deserved it." She comes over to the bed and puts her face near mine. "And it's not going to do any good to go running to Nettie. She's still on parole. If you do anything to ruin this, I'll have her back in prison so fast, she won't know what happened to her."

No more words. Everything's been said. She backs out the door and pulls it closed. I hear her fiddling with the knob and think maybe she's coming back in. But no, in a minute her door closes—more primping for Max. I hear the wind wailing and sleet beating against the window. It wasn't supposed to start this early. Maybe she won't be able to go.

I HEAR THE KITCHEN DOOR slam and run to the window. Aunt Paulina's wrapped in her fur coat, struggling against the wind to take a single step. When she finally reaches the garage, I relax just a little when the doors won't open. But finally they do and before long, I watch as the car backs slowly down the driveway. As soon as she's gone, I head for my door. It's stuck. I try to open it again, harder. The lock! I forgot about the lock. So *that's* what she was doing. She's never used it before. I look for something to break the knob. There's nothing. The Becks' blinds are closed, but maybe if I yell, somebody will hear. When I open the window, the fierceness of the storm attacks me.

The sleet feels like needles against my skin and the freezing wind sounds like a million cats howling. I call Nettie's name until my throat is sore. There's no answer, so I close the window and slide down the wall till I'm sitting on the floor.

> *...I don't see's there's much difference between the Fromes up at the farm and the Fromes down in the graveyard; 'cept that down there they're all quiet, and the women have got to hold their tongues.*

I start the book over and read it again and again until I hear voices in the hall and then Aunt Paulina's door close.

Thirty

THE SUN IS MAKING shadows on my floor when I hear Nettie singing in the hall. She's coming to wake me up and ask what I want for breakfast, the same as she does every morning. I hear the doorknob rattle and then her voice—a little bit frantic. "Kat? Are you in there? I can't open the door. Kat! Answer me."

"She locked it," I say, struggling to push the dresser away from the door.

In a minute I hear the linen closet door slam and then the sound of a key in my lock.

"What happened?" Nettie asks. "Why do you have your coat on?" She looks around the room. "Your bed hasn't been slept in. And why are your suitcases packed?"

"He's back," I say in a whisper.

"Who's back? What are you talking about?"

"Max. She went and got him."

"Oh my god! This time she's gone too far." When she hugs me, her cheek feels like ice. Even her hair is cold. She holds me at arm's length and stares into my eyes. Then, without saying a word, she heads straight for Aunt Paulina's room and pounds on the door so hard, I think she's going to bust right through it.

By the time I get there, Aunt Paulina's standing in the doorway, tying the sash of her robe and aiming her anger at Nettie. "You know better than to wake me up. What's the matter with you?"

"What's the matter with *me*? You're the one who brought that monster back into this house. Have you lost your mind?"

Aunt Paulina's drapes are drawn, but I can see Max get out of bed and head our way. My body feels as if somebody's grabbed hold and is shaking the daylights out of it. Nettie reaches over and takes my hand. She still has her gloves on.

Aunt Paulina starts to close the door, but Nettie pushes it open again. "If you don't get rid of him right this minute, I'm going to the police and tell them what he did."

"The police?" Aunt Paulina's grinning huge. "*You're* going to the police? Well, wait just a minute. I'll get dressed and go with you. It'll be interesting to see what they do when I tell them about all the money that's missing and how you threatened to kill me because I wouldn't give you a raise."

Max is standing beside Aunt Paulina now, and Nettie's hand tightens around my fingers. I am still shaking, but I'm surprised I'm not feeling as sick as I did that horrible night.

Max smiles at Nettie as if everything's the same as it used to be. But he's acting as if I'm not even here. I have to get him to look at me. He owes me at least that much. I glare straight at him. He glances my way for a second before his eyes drop to the ground. Then his face turns somber. "Nobody has to go to the police."

"But, Max," Aunt Paulina says, "they're not going to believe her lies. I'll get her arrested so she won't be able to make any more trouble." She puts her arm through his. "And you didn't *do* anything. It was all a misunderstanding."

He gives Aunt Paulina a long, dark look and says, "You are *not* going to the police." Then he turns and walks back into the dimness.

Now Aunt Paulina's face is somber as she looks at Nettie. "I suppose you want money to keep quiet."

"No. I don't want your money."

"Well, what, then?"

This time I squeeze Nettie's hand while my breath catches in my chest.

She takes a step forward. "I want Kat outright. For good."

Aunt Paulina's body relaxes. "Is that *all?*"

Nettie nods firmly. "That's all."

All of a sudden, I can breathe and I'm not shaking anymore.

I'M STANDING in the hall next to my suitcases, and Nettie's fishing around in the linen closet for the key to Mama's bedroom. "Are you sure you want to do this?" she asks. "There's nothing in there."

"I'm sure." The only piece of Mama that's left in this entire house is in there.

As soon as the door is open, I head for the crawl space in the closet and pull back the piece of loose white wallpaper. Then I rescue one of Mama's lilies and put it in my pocket.

On the way toward the stairs, Nettie says, "Here, let me carry one of those suitcases."

I smile, then shake my head. "You've done enough carrying. Now it's my turn."

As soon as the front door closes behind us, I take in a huge breath of cold air to get the scent of Shalimar out of my nose and hope I never have to smell that fragrance again.

Epilogue

I PRAYED SO HARD that night. That Max would run the car off the road and he and Aunt Paulina would both be killed. But God ignored me. And I'm beginning to understand that you have to let him handle things in his own way, in his own good time—that he knows what he's doing.

I'm living at the Becks' now. Mr. Beck let me have Lily's room. She married the French horn player and they're happy. She mentioned something in one of her letters about having Johnny go out for a visit. But I'll have to wait to see that one with my own eyes before I believe it.

Mrs. Beck's roses are in bloom again, and Mr. Beck is working on a new book. I'm typing it for him, but not when I'm out with David. And remember when I said the thing about there only being one true love for each of us? I believe it as sure as anything.

Aunt Paulina's alone now. Max was only there for about a week. Nettie thinks after I left, he just stayed long enough to sweet-talk her out of another load of money and then moved on. The lawn that used to be manicured perfectly looks like the Becks' did when I first moved to Ellenville. And the only time I see Aunt Paulina come out of the house is when she dumps empty whiskey bottles into the trash barrel beside the garage. I remember the promise I made to make her pay for what she did to Mama. In the end, I didn't have to do anything at all. She did it to herself. That's the sort of thing that makes me sure God is really up there.

And I think how if Mama hadn't died, I would never have known about Nettie. We're sitting under an oak tree in the backyard, going through Mama's keepsake box. These things help me remember where I came from. And that's something everybody should know.